THE

MILKMAN:

BOOK II

GREG BUCK

ISBN: 978-1-7329909-2-0

DEDICATION

To all my friends who have made life
interesting.

ACKNOWLEDGEMENTS

The author would like to thank his wife Lori Buck for her patience and support and of course Katharine Smith, the most extraordinary editor.

Chapter One

It was late May and the summer fairs and amusement parks were open and in full swing. Temperatures were just right for outdoor activities this time of year in Westminster, Colorado. The early evening air was full of high-pitched screams from the girls and boys on the rides, along with the carnival music playing from speakers throughout the fairgrounds. Kids were running around with their cotton candy sticks in hand, looking for new games and their favorite rides.

To the naked eye, the Walker family looked like a typical young, happy American family. Two attractive parents were holding hands and walking along with their pre-teen son and a younger daughter. Ryder Walker had decided on this family outing to the county fair. They would eat roasted turkey legs and junk food for dinner, and enjoy a couple of rides and a few carnival games.

Ryder Walker was the macho, proud type. He did not like to be seen as weak or lesser in any form. His shoulders were wide, his arms were well muscled, and he had a strong aura of confidence about him. He was attractive to the ladies and liked to keep his brown wavy hair long, and show off his tattoos by wearing sleeveless t-shirts.

Entry into the fairgrounds was free and as they made their way through the open gated entrance, Haylee Walker ran ahead to see what was beyond the gates, as any young excited child would. She was nearing six years of age and almost always wore her long blonde hair pulled back into a ponytail. Ryder and Karen were holding hands and strolling along behind, watching the direction Haylee was heading. She would look back a lot to make sure her parents were following her. Trailing behind Ryder and Karen was their son Gary. He had his hands in his pockets, with his head down, and seemed to not be very interested in attending the fair. Most people just figured he was at that age where he was embarrassed to be with his parents in public. He was a tall, slightly overweight kid, with a lighter complexion than his sister and dark brown hair. His parents did not pay attention to him and his sulking ways; they were there to enjoy the evening.

"Mommy! Daddy! Over here," yelled Haylee.

They saw her pointing to the left. She had found the smoked and seasoned turkey leg concession stand. As always, the roasted ear of corn stand was right next to it. Ryder lifted his nose and took in the aroma as they filed into line. Karen and Gary took a couple of steps to the right for the roasted corn line. Ryder and Haylee would grab the turkey legs. They met up under a blooming crabapple tree, about thirty yards away from the two stands. The Walkers sat down on the grass under the tree, with a huge supply of napkins, and began the wonderfully delicious messy process of eating the turkey legs, which were so large that when Haylee would go to take a bite you could not see her face.

There was not much talking while they were working on their carnival feast. As they finished up they each threw their gnawed turkey bone and stripped ear of corn into the trash can and cleaned up with a couple of wet naps. Haylee was anxious to get to the rides. Her favorite was the bumper cars and she knew exactly where that ride was setup.

Haylee grabbed Ryder's hand, "Come on Daddy, the bumper cars are this way."

Karen and Gary followed along behind them, through the crowds of people towards the bumper cars, Gary still sulking and bringing up the rear of the family unit.

They all rode the bumper cars for three different sessions. Ryder had slipped the ride operator an extra ten-dollar bill so they could ride continuously without having to exit the ride and stand back in line. Karen actually saw Gary smile a couple of times and that warmed her heart; he had been through a rough few years.

After the bumper cars they made their way around the rest of the rides, choosing only a couple more to try out as it was getting late. Karen knew that Gary always loved the Zipper ride so she bought him and Haylee a ticket to go ride it. The parents sat this one out and took a seat on a bench. Ryder lit a cigarette. The kids had come back to them already dizzy but Ryder insisted on buying them all tickets for the Spinning Teacup ride. He grabbed the center console and started spinning them relentlessly. Karen and Haylee almost got sick. Gary just sat there with that dull, blank look on his face, all the while they were spinning. Afterwards, Karen told Ryder she would never step foot on that ride with him again.

After they finished with the rides, they had to pass through the carnival gaming area on their way to the parking lot. Haylee noticed a huge stuffed pink elephant hanging off the ceiling of one of the games. This stuffed animal was every bit as big as her.

"Daddy can I have that?" Haylee grabbed his hand and was jumping up and down while pointing at the elephant. Ryder loved his little girl and would do just about anything for her. He looked down at the game and noticed it was the milk bottle toss. The three milk bottles were stacked in a pyramid, with one balanced on top of the two on the bottom. There were three baseballs sitting on a felt counter, about ten feet away from the milk bottles. Ryder stepped up and purchased one game which meant he got the three balls.

The carnival game operator told him, "You have to knock all three bottles down for that big elephant."

Ryder picked one up and reared his arm back, throwing the ball incredibly hard. It hit just to the left of the lower bottles. He threw the second one and knew he had over-compensated the second he released it. This one hit to the right of the lower bottles. His last ball went low and hit the table in front of the milk bottles. They visibly shook but none of them fell down. He was now determined and checked his wallet; he had enough cash for three more games. The second game, all three of his throws went wide right. He seemed to be getting worse. The third game, he was throwing high, and by the time he had spent the rest of his cash his throws were noticeably softer. Not one time did he even graze a single milk bottle with a baseball.

The game operator lightly lofted one of the baseballs to Gary and said, "Come on kid, give it a try. This one is on me."

Ryder looked at Gary with his sideways glare. Gary did not notice the look and he stepped up to the felt table. He pulled back and threw the ball as hard as he could at the milk bottles, hitting directly in the middle of the lower two bottles. All three bottles exploded and fell to the table.

Haylee let out a yelp and jumped for glee, "All right, Gary! Nice throw!"

She ran over to the table while the game operator was pulling out a small step ladder and reaching up to release the ties on the large stuffed pink elephant. Haylee gave her brother a big hug, "Thank you." She was ecstatic with her new stuffed animal. Showing it off and hugging it. She kept talking about it as they were all walking back to the car to go home. Ryder had said it was time to go; he was out of money.

They got out to the gravel parking lot and as the lights from the fairgrounds did not extend this far, it was dark. Ryder had to stop for a second to let his eyes adjust so he could find their dark grey Nissan Altima. He finally spotted it and his family followed him over to the car.

Ryder said softly to Gary, "Wait right there."

He pulled out the keys and opened the car for Karen and Haylee. He started the car and put on some music then stepped back out of the car. Gary was standing in place with his head down. He knew what was about to happen. Ryder pointed to the back of the car and Gary turned and started slowly walking around to the back of the Altima. Before he rounded the rear fender by the trunk, he felt a foot smash into the middle of his back and he went flying forward, into a patch of tall grass. As he was lying face-down in the grass he felt two more hard slugs, one into each side of his ribs. They were painful, but not the worst he had ever received from Ryder.

Ryder said, "What did I tell you about making a fool out of me?"

Gary grunted, "Sorry." Because he knew from experience that it was better to answer him than to remain silent.

"Get your ass up, boy."

Gary feebly rose up to his knees then proceeded to slowly stand while grimacing and holding his right side. Ryder had popped the trunk when he unlocked the doors to the car for the women. He walked over and lifted the trunk hood up. "You know the drill."

Gary shuffled over to the trunk opening and was starting to crawl in when Ryder pushed him, "Hurry up, you retard!" Once he landed in the trunk with a hard thud and banged his elbow on the tire iron, Gary turned to look at Ryder, who was shaking his head and smiling. Then Ryder grabbed the top of the trunk lid, slammed it shut, nonchalantly walked around the car to the driver's side door, got in and drove off.

Chapter Two

Raven Elizabeth Martin was sitting on a picnic table with a red solo cup of Coors light beer in her hand, talking with a couple of her friends. One of them was John's girlfriend, Melissa Baxter, who was sitting on the picnic table next to her. They were reminiscing and laughing about some of the things that happened during their high-school years.

The afternoon was warm and the sun felt good on Raven's face. About fifty feet away, John Rodney and Jesse were standing next to Old Blue. The hood was up and several guys were standing near, admiring the refurbished 1968 Pontiac Firebird. It still needed a paint job but mechanically it was sound and it sure sounded like a hot rod. Jesse, with John's help, replaced the original motor with a powerful 400-cubic-inch motor that was rated to push out 335 horsepower. He was proud of this Firebird that he and his father Aaron had started restoring years ago. After Aaron had passed away in a car accident five years before, Jesse had to continue the project on his own, with his friend John's help.

Jesse Hardner was twenty-two now. Not a lot had changed in his life over the last three years; he still worked at Romans' Dairy as a delivery driver; he still lived with his mom, Becky, and he was still dating Raven. Most of the men at the party remembered her nickname in high school and still called her Ravishing Raven. Jesse would just smile when he heard this nickname. He was proud of her too and agreed that she was ravishing. She had a perfectly formed figure, long black hair and emerald-green eyes. Her almost milky-white complexion seemed to highlight her other features.

The one thing that had changed significantly for Jesse was that he had completed an associate's degree in electrical technology and was now pursuing a bachelor's degree in electrical engineering.

It had only been four years since his class had graduated high school, so instead of a formal party which usually occurred every five years, a few of his old classmates had the idea to start having a big outdoor party each year in late May, when the weather was just right to celebrate outside. This year they were at the vast Golden Gate Canyon State Park; about fourteen miles northwest of Golden Colorado, in the foothills above the city. You could enjoy any number of recreational activities there, including fishing, hunting, hiking, bird and wildlife-watching.

Where they were hanging out, the road was graveled, but there was a large area with a huge red barn for shelter and picnic tables spread about. Loud music was playing from somebody's open car doors in the parking area, just loud enough for all to hear.

There were three large kegs of Coors Banquet beer and two large kegs of Coors Light, sitting near the entrance to the red barn, several of the guys hanging around them. Raven called them the keg guardians. They were never far away from the beer and if you showed up with an empty red solo cup they would fill it up; you just had to specify your preferred flavor. The keg guardians would always be arguing amongst themselves about how much air pressure needed to be pumped into a particular keg for the beer to flow properly.

There was a little grassy section on the south side of the red barn, which had been turned into a dancing area. On the other side of the barn, some people had setup a couple of temporary horse-shoe pits. Similar to a pool hall, some people were standing around watching the game, waiting their turn. Quite often, you would hear a *clank,* as a shoe bounced off a post, then a response from the crowd. Just beyond the horse-shoe pits, there was another group of people throwing a Frisbee back and forth. The majority of the people were standing around the picnic bench area, beers in hand, just talking. Some of the guys were in the parking lot, showing off their cars. There was such a big turnout that the keg guardians decided to only charge fifty cents per beer. They were not in the business of making money. They just wanted to break even.

Jesse had agreed to drive so he kept his beer count way down. John, on the other hand, acted like he was in some kind of drinking competition and was double-fisted with red solo cups most of the afternoon. John would rather walk home or sleep against a tree with his butt on the ground than be told he could only have four Coors Banquet beers at a reunion party, or any party for that matter. Raven and Melissa, would each have a few but they never did drink too much.

After showing off his car to his old classmates, Jesse grabbed Raven's hand and they walked over to the horse-shoe pits and played a couple of games against another couple. John and Melissa remained near the picnic tables, talking to a group of friends and old classmates. John was getting quite boisterous.

In high school, Jesse had a reputation as one of the tougher kids. With that stigma came the chance that another may want to challenge him to a fight so they could see how they measured up against him. John, was a different story. Nobody messed with him throughout high school. He made sure of that by taking out the senior bully when he was a freshman. John also had an aura about him that made people respect him and not press the issue.

This bully that John beat up several years ago had a younger brother, in their high school class. Jesse spotted Tommy Dubron sitting on the tailgate of his 1990 Ford F150 pickup with a few friends. He was constantly looking over and watching John. It was a known fact that Tommy's brother, Bobby, held a grudge and was still pretty upset about the whole ordeal and he had been looking to get even. Jesse did not see Bobby amongst the crowd but Tommy could be running point. Last year at this same reunion party, Jesse remembered talking to Tommy for a while and how surprised Tommy acted when John and he had shown up.

Golden Gate Canyon Park was known for large outdoor parties and it closed an hour after sundown. Right on queue at 9:30 PM, two Jefferson County sheriff cars rolled into the gravel parking lot. They got out of their cars and started telling the crowd that it was time to pack up and disperse. The crowd let out a few boos, but they all started to obey and pack up.

One of the deputies happened to be Peters. He had been with the Westminster City police department the last time Jesse had run into him. Deputy Peters noticed John and Jesse as they were starting to open the Firebird and put away the blankets and other item they had brought. He made his way over and shook hands with them, introducing his new partner. There was not much eye contact; they were definitely on duty. Both of the deputies were a little busy eyeing the crowd and looking for anyone too inebriated to drive.

Deputy Peters kind of frowned at John and said, "John, you are not driving, are you?"

Jesse answered, "No sir, he is riding with me."

Deputy Peters nodded his head and then stepped over in front of a few guys that were piling into the car next to Jesse's. He took the keys from the driver and looked closely at the other three then handed the keys to one of the others. Then he walked over, stood up on one of the picnic tables so all could see him and addressed the crowd.

"I see a lot of work went into this party with the canopies, kegs and horse-shoe pits. We are going to leave now and we will be back in one hour. Everyone and everything needs to be gone." He gave Jesse a slight wave then the deputies all moved to their cars and drove away.

Jesse and John stuck around to help people load up and get on their way. They were the last ones to leave the parking lot. He noticed that Tommy Dubron's gang had been one of the first to leave. It looked like there were about eleven of them by the time the party was over. John sat in the backseat with Melissa, he was too drunk to even be co-pilot. He laid his head against his girlfriend's shoulder and was near snoring before they got out of the parking lot. Raven was in the passenger seat, fully awake and aware. She was mentioning a couple of her friends that she had talked to tonight for the first time since the graduation ceremony.

"Well that was fun! Where does the time go? Three years and I have not seen or spoken to Camille and Rhonda."

Melissa replied, "I know, and it seems like most of the guys still haven't become men." Both Melissa and Raven chuckled.

All of the cars were heading south and east on Crawford Gulch road, to exit the park and make the descent down the foothills back to the city. The pine tree lined dirt road was narrow and Jesse was driving about five miles-per-hour over the suggested speed limit. They came around a corner and saw a few cars in front of them, stopped with their brake lights on.

Jesse said, "What is Sam doing in the road? They left twenty minutes ago."

The Dubron brothers, along with their crew of eleven cronies, had decided to set up a blockade a couple of miles down the road from the party location. The spot they chose was rock and tree-lined, and there was no way to get around the blockade. Jesse watched the car in front of them. Sam, one of Bobby Dubron's self-proclaimed henchmen, was slowing the car down to a stop by stepping out in front of each car as they were approaching. Like a deer in headlights. Jesse thought that was a rather stupid thing to do, considering the amount of alcohol that was consumed in the park by these same drivers. Sam Hart walked up, looked in the car and said a few words. Then he tapped the top of the car and the driver took off.

Jesse just now realized what was happening. The blockade consisted of a car on each side of the road, with a driver in both cars, and they were close enough to only allow a single vehicle through. He looked over to the left and saw Bobby sitting next to Tommy on the tailgate of his truck. There were a dozen other guys standing around doing Bobby's bidding. They were looking for John. Fortunately, John was snoring in the backseat.

Raven asked, "What's going on, Jesse? For a minute I thought it was a DUI checkpoint set up by those deputies."

"Do you guys have a blanket or coat, or something to throw over John's face?"

Both of the women looked at Jesse curiously. Then Melissa said, "No, I think we put all of that gear in the trunk."

Jesse pulled forward and Sam stepped out into the road in front of the Firebird with his hand out, signaling for Jesse to stop. He walked around to the driver's window and looked inside. Jesse could feel the cool of the late spring air in his nostrils and was fully aware of the danger before him. He was paying attention to every little detail.

"Hey Sam, what's up?"

"Yo, Jesse. Who's in the car with you?" As he said that, Sam dipped his head to look into the back seat. He stood straight back up and said out loud, "We got John here!"

Jesse saw Bobby stand up and thought to himself that even in John's drunken state he could probably take out four of them, but there are at least a dozen guys. That left eight for him.

Sam gestured for Jesse to get out of the car. "Come on Jesse, get out. We just want to talk to John for a minute."

Jesse looked around and noticed Bobby was getting closer to the car while Tommy was instructing two other cars to block the road ahead of them.

"He's too drunk, Sam. He's not getting out of this car."

Sam took a step closer to the driver side door, pulled his right arm back and slugged Jesse on the left side of his face. Raven and Melissa screamed. Jesse's head just dipped and turned a little to the right. Sam went to pull his arm back out of the car and realized there was no give; his arm was stuck. He looked down to see Jesse staring at him. There was no humor in those eyes.

Jesse said in a low guttural voice, "You shouldn't have done that Sam."

Then he gunned the Firebird, still holding onto Sam's forearm. The two cars were closing the gap and Jesse didn't want to let them lock him in place. Sam screamed and fell out of view immediately, but Jesse knew he was still there; he was holding his right forearm. He could also feel the pull of Sam's feet and legs being dragged across the dirt road and into the ditch next to it. There was a little resistance and a grunt from Sam with each rock and branch he was pulled over. Right after the Firebird cleared where the two cars were trying to block them in, Jesse pushed Sam's forearm away from the vehicle so he wouldn't get caught under the rear tires. He watched in the side view mirror as Sam rolled into the ditch and he just lay still in a balled-up heap.

Due to the way Jesse had to gun the Firebird and leave the scene, there was a huge cloud of thick dust that hung in the air behind him. He tried to look through all of the dust in the rear-view mirror and he thought he saw that the two blockers collided in the middle of the road. It looked like the headlights of each car were resting against one another and maybe a little steam was rising from their hoods, but it was hard to tell looking through all of that dust.

"Raven, are there any lights following us?"

She was turned around in her seat and looking out the back window. She leaned over and kissed him on the cheek then settled back in her seat. There was a big smile on her face. "Not a one. Great thinking! You're my Superman!"

Jesse looked in the rear-view mirror again and saw Melissa's huge brown eyes looking at him. John was still asleep.

Chapter Three

Gary Walker had been born to a different father than his half-sister Haylee, but he had taken Ryder's name to please his new stepfather. His biological father's name was Doug. Doug still lived in the area but rarely had anything to do with his only child. He was known locally as the town drunk. There was a set of four different bars within a half mile of Doug's apartment and if he was not at home, he was surely to be belly up at one of these bars. He never remembered Gary's birthday and seldom bought him a gift for Christmas. It had been two years since Doug had bothered to contact his son.

Ryder Walker and Doug had been good friends years ago, before Doug met Karen. Ryder had fallen for Karen before Doug had even proposed to her. She had always flirted with Ryder and Doug had seen it plenty of times. Ryder was very handsome and charismatic and women were always drawn to him.

Doug and Karen had their ups and downs, as lots of newly-weds do, and during one of these downs Ryder was able to step in and lead Karen away. This had happened about six years ago and Doug was still having a hard time coping with the loss of his family. He blamed everyone else for this loss and would not accept that he drove Karen away. Karen had truly loved Doug in the beginning but as time went by he seemed to grow more and more distant from her and would really only pay attention to Gary. He would attend Gary's sporting events and always helped him with his homework. They would go out back and throw a baseball or football and Doug loved to take his son to the ice-cream shop for a couple of vanilla cones. In the meantime, Doug had forgotten Karen's birthday one year and he always forgot their anniversary. He never exhibited any remorse or sorrow, either. Karen truly thought he was stepping away because he had found somebody else, even though he denied it continually. That thought made it easier for Karen to break it off.

Karen was surprised and hugely disappointed when Doug started to distance himself from Gary afterwards. She figured that would be the case between the two of them, especially since her new beau was a former friend of Doug's. However, she had never expected that to happen between Doug and his only child. It was not long after she got together with Ryder that she became pregnant, driving a wedge even further into her relationship with her ex. The final straw for Doug and Gary's relationship was three years ago, when Ryder pretty much forced Gary to take his last name. Ryder said he wanted everyone to think their family unit was whole and there were only two parents involved.

Shortly after the name-change was final, Doug showed up on the Walkers' front porch one night. He was extremely drunk and holding a baseball bat. Doug started spurting off and yelling about how he wanted the little boy he used to protect to step outside and meet his maker. Karen was not sure what he was talking about and took it for drunken gibberish. Then there was a loud crash on the front porch and she looked through a window to see that Doug had smashed their Romans' Dairy milk box into tiny pieces. He yelled and pounded on the door for a couple more minutes and then she watched him stumble off the porch, down the sidewalk, dragging the bat behind him in the direction of his apartment. Ryder was not home during this escapade and Karen was thankful, for that would have turned into a frightful brawl.

Chapter Four

It was Monday morning and Jesse's alarm went off at 2:30 AM. He sat up a little slower than usual, realizing he had a little bit of a hangover from the reunion party. His clothes and shoes were sitting on the chair next to him. He managed to get dressed and walked on out to the kitchen, searching for a coffee cup. Just over the last year he had developed a taste and an almost need for coffee in the morning. He only required two mugs a day, though.

Jesse still rode his broken-down ten-speed bicycle to work each day unless the weather dictated otherwise. He felt it gave him a little bit of exercise and time to think about his life as he rode. The derailleur on his Schwinn was still broken and the bike was stuck in seventh gear. It made starting the ride a little tough, but once you got it up to speed, seventh was the perfect gear. Jesse's home was on a downhill slope, which helped to get up to speed on the initial launch. After his first cup of coffee, he stepped outside onto the porch and reached with his right hand behind the evergreen bush that ran along the concrete walkway and pulled out his bike. His second cup of coffee was always in a to-go thermos that he drank while driving his delivery route. Against his mother's wishes, he always stowed his bike behind the evergreen bush in the front yard. Only one time was it stolen from behind the bush and Jesse had found it abandoned a few blocks away, in a field. He figured the thief did not enjoy having only seventh gear available.

There were a few options in routes he could take to get to his place of employment at Romans' Dairy. His ride to work was a little over two miles, unless he decided to take the rural route. This rural route was close to eight miles and ran along a few dirt roads, through a sparsely populated area just west of the city. The city lights were not as intrusive, which made the stars brighter, and there was always a chance of seeing, or in Jesse's experience, running into wildlife. This morning he decided to take the rural route and hopefully work some of the cobwebs out of his mind.

His bike had just left the pavement and dropped an inch or so down onto the dirt road. This is where the city was left behind. The moon was bright this morning so he could see a good distance ahead on the road, and to the sides, out into the high prairie fields of grass. This morning, he saw a big buck mule deer and a few scampering coyotes as he rode along. It was quiet; none of the coyotes wanted to yip or howl as he rode by.

He pulled into the large gravel lot at Romans' Dairy. He saw Mr. Jerry Roman through the window of his office in the front of the house, talking on the phone and waving his arms around as he was pacing about. Several of the other delivery trucks were already idling in the parking area. Drivers had finished loading up their delivery goods and were warming up their trucks to begin their delivery routes.

Jesse walked over and pulled the customer order list off the dash of his truck. Mr. Roman had put a yellow sticky on the list that said, 'You'll need to go see Linda and gas up.' He sighed and put the sticky note on the dash and started loading his truck with today's customer order list. Jesse still referred to Jerry as Mr. Roman. He has known him ever since he could remember, as an old family friend.

After he was done loading up the custom crates in back, which Mr. Roman had built, he jumped in the driver's seat and started back towards the city he had just left. The gas station was at the far end of his delivery route from the dairy, which was perfect for the course he liked to take. When delivering, Jesse liked to drive out to the furthest delivery point and work his way back towards the dairy. He pulled into the gas station and noticed Linda was all alone inside the store. He was going to have to listen to a story.

"Good morning, Linda."

She looked up from the newspaper she was reading, "There's that sexy man. How's it going, Jesse?"

Linda stood up and smiled at Jesse. He returned the smile.

"Doing good here. How are you, Linda?"

"Same old, same old. Bored, broke and hungry."

Jesse smiled again, "I need to fill up that truck on Mr. Roman's account."

"I got ya, pump number seven it is."

Jesse thought he was going to get out of the store without having to listen to a long, drawn-out story. He started to turn around and was getting ready to say goodbye when Linda looked at him, "So, Jesse. There is a rumor going around about someone in an old Firebird dragging one of his classmates down the road a ways by his arm. It seems that this guy decided to punch the driver of the Firebird while he was sitting behind the wheel and then the driver grabbed his arm and drug him along the road for a while. The driver of the Pontiac got away and the other feller ended up with some severe road rash scrapes and was treated at the urgent

care clinic. He wouldn't say who the driver was
or press charges." She paused at that point.

Jesse replied, "Interesting. Well, it sounds
like that guy got what he deserved."

Her mouth fell open. "Is that all you have
to say about this, Jesse?"

"You know me, Linda. I don't like to kiss
and tell." He smiled and backed out through
the glass door.

Jesse filled up his truck, put it in gear, then
headed for his delivery area. Street by street,
block by block, he made his way through the
neighborhood. Verifying the customer's order
against his clipboard and then usually jogging to
their porch and placing the order in the milk
box. However, most people would put their
used milk bottles in the milk box, which meant
he would have to stop and put their current
order down on the porch and pull out all of the
recyclables. Then he would have to regather the
current order and place it into the milk box.
Once in a while, he would come across a
customer who would leave their recyclables on
the side next to the milk box, and that was
always appreciated. Then he would jog back to
the truck. Since it was nearing the beginning of
summer, about half way through his route the
sun would be starting to rise. There were
people waving and saying 'Hi'. Some of them
were customers out and about on their early
morning jogs, or walking with their dogs. This

had always been a friendly neighborhood and Jesse was proud and happy to have grown up nearby.

Jesse had finished his route and was backing up to his stall, along the long, flat wooden deck where he loaded and unloaded his truck each day. He first pulled off all of the recyclable items, like the glass milk bottles, pie tins and juice jugs. These were to be put on the sidewalk next to the Romans' house. Mrs. Roman - Fran - would rinse them out and run them through a commercial dishwasher that would sterilize all of the recyclables. Since they had their logo etched onto the bottles, jugs and pie tins, they did not have to worry about it being washed off or faded. After the recyclables were unloaded, the rest of the truck would need to be unloaded into the cooling locker, right behind where each truck parked. Mr. Roman would come out and take inventory each afternoon and determine what could be kept and what needed to be tossed. The whole structure with the loading deck and cooling lockers resembled a long line of covered horse stalls.

After he had finished unloading his truck, Jesse was walking toward his bike and noticed the care basket sitting next to it. Fran left a care basket next to his bike for him and his mother, Becky, to enjoy brunch together each morning. This practice started the year Jesse's father had died; the automotive accident had also put his mom in a wheelchair for a while. Becky was out of the wheelchair now, but used a cane when she walked. Jesse mounted his bike and picked up the care basket to put it under his left arm. Fran was looking at him through the big window near their kitchen table where they usually ate. He waved and smiled; Fran returned both gestures.

In one fluid motion, Jesse dismounted his bike in the driveway, still holding the care basket under his left arm, picked up the Schwinn with his right hand and placed it behind the evergreen bush. As he approached the front door he heard Drew Carey's voice and then it sounded like the music for the Cliff Hangers game was playing. This was a cardboard game with a mountain as the background and a little mountain-climber that walked up a mountain slope to an Old Swedish Mountain music song, *On The Franches*. His mom continually informed him of all kinds of useless game show trivia.

He opened the door and stepped in. "Good morning, Ma."

Becky looked over, "Good morning, Jesse. This guy just way overbid on that blender and he's gonna send the climber over the cliff."

"Well, they oughta just start throwing tomatoes at him then!"

"I bet his wife does when he gets home. Two hundred dollars for a blender. My word."

"I have smelled homemade biscuits under this towel since I started my ride home and my belly is growling now. I'm going to the kitchen. Be back in a minute." Jesse lifted off the towel from the care basket and saw four large biscuits and two lidded carafes. One carafe was holding orange juice and the other looked to be sausage gravy. This was one of Jesse's favorite breakfasts. His mom always called it brunch, since it was after nine in the morning when they ate. He pulled out a couple of plates and put two buttered biscuits on each then smothered them with the gravy. He poured two large glasses of orange juice and carried them over to the small kitchen table.

Becky had already moved from the couch to the table, in anticipation of brunch.

She smiled when the plates were put down, "Fran's biscuits and gravy are the best. Yummy time!"

Since *The Price Is Right* had gone to commercial, Jesse knew this was the time to talk to his game show loving mother. "So, what's on the agenda today?"

"Well, the girls have invited me to join them bowling today. I have not tried to bowl in over five years."

"That sounds great, Ma."

"I am looking forward to it. I do want to be home by 3:00 PM though, when *Let's Make a Deal* starts."

"You will be. Go enjoy some time with your friends."

The commercials had ended and Drew Carey was once again on the screen. Becky turned back to the television, watching intently. Jesse slopped up the last of the gravy onto his plate and took his setting out to the kitchen to wash it off.

Chapter Five

Even though most of the other kids are out of
school for summer break, this morning Gary
was getting ready for summer school. Gary
used to consistently get high marks in school; he
was an intelligent boy. His grades had been
deteriorating over the last few years and this
time he needed to make up a course during the
summer break. Actually, he was happy to have
a place to go. It got him away from home and
Ryder for the day. For years, Karen had to dress
Gary in a turtle-neck, to hide any bruises. She
had bought rouge that matched Gary's
complexion and she would rub it on any bruises
which could not be covered by clothing. Gary
continued dressing in this pattern as he was
growing up; very seldom was he seen wearing a
t-shirt. He would be turning thirteen in a couple
of months and could not wait until he was old
enough to move out, if he made it that long. He

had only one friend, besides his sister, who he could trust.

Jeremy Olsen had just turned thirteen and he was considered a nerd by his classmates. He had known Gary for seven years and he remembered when he used to get good grades and he wasn't so depressed all of the time. Jeremy was fully aware of the beatings that Ryder punished Gary with, but Gary always pleaded with him to not say anything to anyone. He was worried about the fate of his sister and his mom if the authorities started to interfere. Gary had told Jeremy, that for the time being, he would take these beatings to keep Ryder away from his mom and sister.

Gary liked hanging out at Jeremy's home. They would play video games in his room, which was sequestered in the basement. Jeremy's nice mom, Tonya, would bring down snacks for them once in a while, including his favorite, pizza rolls. She was also a great chef and at times he was invited to stay for dinner. He never passed up that invitation. For one thing, he was never sure if he would get a meal when he got home; it depended on how drunk his mom got during the day. Also, he would do almost anything to avoid Ryder.

Jeremy also had a fifteen-year-old sister who Gary thought was beautiful and she would talk to him once in a while. Most girls shied away from Gary, because of his depression and quietness. But Brenda Olsen would sit down next to him and make small talk. She would ask him how his day was and how things were at school and home; questions his mom never even asked him anymore, not since the drinking began. Once Jeremy would pull out his game consoles and start setting up a game, Brenda would always walk away and go to her room or the kitchen and talk with her mom and dad. She did not care about video games. Gary played more to appease Jeremy than himself. He would sometimes sneak out to the kitchen when Jeremy was busy setting up and talk to the Olsens. They were a nice family that engaged him in conversation without any type of threat.

A few, times Gary knew he had caught the Olsens discussing something related to his home life. There would be whispering and the subject would change when he entered the kitchen. Jeremy swore he had never told his parents anything, but Tonya was suspicious that something was not quite right within the Walkers' home. Gary would show up on their doorstep at times, sad, with new bruises. She would ask questions, but he would evade the subject and hide what she knew was the truth.

Tonya also thought that as well as becoming more and more guarded, Gary was losing weight. She had asked the boys to go play at Gary's home many times, but always received an excuse as to why they could not.

Not once could she recall her son visiting the Walkers' home but she thought he must have at some point. She talked this over with her husband a couple of times. He only had two answers that he would regurgitate, while keeping his nose in the newspaper, kicked back in his recliner. There was the ever-popular "It's none of our business," or the less popular "It's called tough love, something that is lacking around here." Tonya would just shake her head at Dave's phrases and lack of interest.

She decided it would be best to keep an eye on Gary and make him comfortable; maybe then he would open up, in a friendly situation. Besides, Brenda already had his attention; Gary was smitten with her presence, worse than a little puppy. His eyes would brighten up when she would speak to him or enter the room.

Once Jeremy had told Tonya that Gary was going to summer school, she became more concerned. The school would not release any information when she called them as a concerned parent. Little did she know that Gary had dropped his grades on purpose, in order to avoid more time at home. Even if it was just for the few hours in the morning before his stepfather left for work.

Chapter Six

Nick and Wanda Hamlin were doing their best to raise three rowdy boys in Lakewood, Colorado.

Terry was a couple years older than Doug, who was a few years older than Harry. Wanda Hamlin had previously been married to another man. He was a sergeant in the army when his squad was ambushed. No one had survived. Wanda was pregnant with Terry when she had received the news.

She met Nick at a mutual friend's house-warming party, while she was pregnant with Terry. She was truly surprised that Nick loved her enough to stay with her through a pregnancy and then help raise another man's son. Doug and Harry were both Nick's sons. In the beginning, Nick had raised Terry as one of his own, but that began to slowly change after his own sons were born.

Nick was a construction foreman for a large house-building company. He brought home a decent enough salary, which enabled Wanda to run a small catering company, but mostly to raise their three boys and keep a clean home. She truly enjoyed raising them, even though they would drive her crazy at times. It was unreal to her how dirty a boy could get in a manner of minutes. Sticks, pine cones, twigs and dirt were attracted to her boys. It didn't matter if they were playing in a clean gymnasium or attending a church sermon, these boys would get dirty.

The local Boy Scout troop Scoutmaster decided to become a snowbird and moved to a warmer climate, in Phoenix, Arizona. With his and Wanda's three boys active in various levels of scouting, Nick decided to take the helm. He enjoyed leading kids and being a foreman. He seemed perfectly suited for the job.

Being a lover of the outdoors and the recreation it contained, Nick would take the troop on camping trips that involved backpacking into a remote area on Friday afternoon and returning on Sunday evening. He would teach them how to start fires, wilderness survival, and the basics of orienteering. Other hobbyists; usually parents of children within the troop, would join and teach the kids about predetermined subjects. These included bird-watching, fishing and archery, but the list was extensive on the different subjects that were explored.

Nick had now been the scoutmaster for a couple of years. He decided, along with a few of the fathers in the troop that regularly joined the camping trips, they would hike with the troop to a pristine lake, full of trout. They loved this prospect, knowing the wives would be fine with them taking this fishing trip. Each of them had a lake to suggest.

Nick pulled off his ball cap, turned it upside-down. "OK, everyone write two lake names on a piece of paper and drop them in."

Of the eight pieces of paper, Jim pulled out 'Round Mountain Lake'. Of course, this happened to be one of Nick's suggestions.

"Great. You guys are gonna love this one. Only about a two-mile bushwhack, there is no trail, but it is relatively flat and always vacant. Besides rainbow trout, it also contains fourteen-inch Brookies."

"Where's it at?" asked Jim.

"Between Steamboat Springs and Walden, about fifteen miles off the pavement, up a forest road. That is the best spot to park to access the lake. Let's leave around noon on Friday, as usual. We should have the tents up and be fishing by 4:00 PM, gentlemen."

"Sounds great, Nick," replied Steve.

Jim drove the van, which was full of equipment and carried nine scouts. Steve was in his pickup with his son and his friend. Nick led the way in his convertible 1964 Ford Thunderbird, transporting the beer, along with his three boys. They had to slow considerably when they got to the forest road. It was full of pot holes, deep ruts and tight turns. Using a car with such low ground clearance, Nick had to make sure of each tire's track on the road. There was no parking lot; Nick found a wide enough spot in the road to park all three vehicles and allow another to pass.

As they tightened down their packs full of supplies, they were all in high spirits at the prospect of a remote high country lake. Fishing gear, tents, sleeping bags and food were all packed in by the scouts. Nick and the other men had the extra burden of beer, which they agreed would be well worth the effort.

Most of the tents were pitched by 4:00 PM, as promised. They chose a spot next to an old rock fire ring that Nick had made a couple years before and there was a fair amount of wood gathered already. Nick gave instructions to the scouts then alleviated himself from camp preparedness. Grabbing a fishing rod, along with two beers for his jacket pockets and one in hand, he headed towards the lake. Steve and Jim were not far behind.

The afternoon was a beautiful bluebird day, with no wind. Temperatures were in the low sixties and only a few clouds were whispering above. The three men found a series of three rocks, about ten feet apart, which they commandeered. Jim tossed his line out, catching a nice brook trout on his first cast. They had brought hot dogs and beans to cook over the fire; the addition of a few fish would be tasty.

Saturday was an identical bluebird day. The troop converged on the lake with their fishing gear. Nick did not get to fish much during the day; he was busy helping with knots and snags and showing them how to release fish back into the lake properly. He allowed each boy to keep one fish for their dinner that night. There was no use in keeping a huge allotment, with no ice and a two-mile hike out.

Most of the scouts were done fishing within a few hours and wanted to move onto something else. Jim took them into the woods to identify various plants, trees and animal tracks. There was a large herd of elk in a meadow that got the scouts excited. After a couple of hours, they made their way back to camp.

Jim heard Steve and Nick laughing down by the lake. Grabbing his fishing gear, he walked to meet them back at the rocks, noticing the whole stash of beer was at their feet in the cool water. The three of them fished the rest of the evening, while the scouts were playing various games around camp. A few of the scouts that had fishing finesse would show up in spots along the rocky shore line, tossing and retrieving their lures; once in a while, a trout.

Full beer cans were heavy to carry back, so it was up to this last night to polish the rest of them off. Nick was already a little tipsy. He had fallen face-first into the lake while releasing a fish, laughing so hard that Jim had to get up to help him back to his rock. Nick was soaked head to toe but continued to fish and drink. This display was nothing new; the scouts had all seen this before.

Nick awoke to the sounds of clanking cast iron and the smell of coffee. His head was pounding and he could not remember much about the previous night. *The lake, I fell in the lake.* He definitely was unaware of how he came to be in this tent, stuffed inside a sleeping bag. To his disbelief he was only wearing a pair of briefs. Looking around, he noticed his clothes were not in the tent. He rolled out of the sleeping bag, crawling over and unzipped the fly to look outside. The first thing that hit him was how bright the sun was, then the pounding in his head increased. Nick looked through squinted eyes, noticing his clothes were strewn about in front of the tent, his pants being the furthest away. *What the hell?*

Pushing the fly zipper all the way up, Nick crawled out of the tent and started to stand. His right foot caught the underside of a tree root, which set him off balance. Face-first, he stumbled into the dirt and pinecones then splayed out on the ground with a grunt. All that the others could see was a man laid out with limbs extended, face-down and wearing only underwear.

Terry dropped on the ground, holding his stomach and laughing. A couple of the others started to snicker but soon looked away when they saw the angered expression on Nick's face. Terry continued laughing and rolling on the ground, he was so caught up in it and didn't realize he was the only one laughing.

Nick stood up, pulled on his pants then brushed himself off. He stepped over to where Terry was carrying on and looked down at him. "What the hell are you laughing at, boy?"

Terry came out of his trance, sat up and looked around at everyone staring in his direction. "Umm… sorry, Dad."

Nick seemed to shrug off the insult and instructed the troop that after breakfast they had four hours to fish or do whatever before it was time to pack up camp. While the scouts were out enjoying their four-hour recess, Nick crawled back into his tent to catch up on some much-needed sleep. He snapped awake when he heard voices filtering back into camp.

Back to the vehicles, they made it just as dark was settling in. Everyone had their head-lamps on, searching for a place to set down their packs. Nick waited until the last of the stragglers had shown up then addressed the crowd.

"I'm going to make this short since we are running late. Did everyone have a good time?"

He got a resounding, "Yes, Mr. Hamlin!" Some of them trailed in a 'Thanks'.

"OK, great trip everyone, and thanks for your cooperation. Now let's get home."

Jim had managed to turn the van around and get it heading in the right direction. Steve backed his truck up into the trees over a stump and turned it around in one fell swoop. He obviously did not care about scratches in the truck's paint job. Terry was standing by the trunk he had just opened in the dark. He had his back to Nick and his brothers pulling off his backpack. Nick walked briskly over and grabbed Terry by the nape of his neck, slammed his head into the bottom of the trunk, then reached down with one hand, grabbing a knee and flipping Terry backside-first into the trunk.

"What the hell, man! That hurt!" Terry yelled.

"Don't you ever embarrass me again, especially in public!" Nick said matter-of-factly, as he slammed the trunk shut.

Terry pounded on the trunk for a minute, "Let me out!"

Nick looked at the two sons he had raised since birth, "Throw your crap in the back seat and jump in."

Harry and Doug minded their father without question or comment. It was a long drive home. At one point, Nick had sped up and was getting a little closer to Jim and Steve. He slowed back down and trailed behind the caravan, at a distance. The other men may wonder why there were only three heads in the car.

Chapter Seven

Sunday finally rolled around and Jesse was looking forward to the afternoon. Not only was this his only day off, but he had a date with Raven and they were meeting at Inspiration Point Park around noon. There is an old metal park bench that is shaded by a beautiful honey locust tree on the north-facing slope of the park. They had been meeting there for dates and to hang out since they started dating five years ago. The whole city of Denver and the outlying foothills are visible from this bench. Now that Jesse had the Firebird running, once in a while they would take that if they wanted to go on a date in a different part of town, or if the weather was foul. However, this was the first weekend of June, and that meant it was opening weekend at Lakeside Amusement Park.

    Lakeside was a small amusement park by today's standards, but it had some great rides and resides on the edge of the picture-perfect Rhoda Lake. Lakeside was family-owned and had been operating at the same location since 1908. It was filled with a lot of history and it still maintained a very old carousel, the likes of which you will not see anywhere else. Many of the animal figures were created by the original wood carver.

Jesse decided to ride his bike this time to Inspiration Point and meet Raven. That way, he did not have to deal with parking a vehicle. It was only about four miles away and took him under fifteen minutes. He pulled his bike out from behind the evergreen bush next to the front door. As he rounded the corner where Inspiration Point Park would become visible, he saw Raven sitting on the bench already waiting for him. She saw him pedaling up the hill and smiled. Jesse approached the bench at a rather high rate of speed. Right before he hit the bench with his front tire, he jumped onto the side of the bench that Raven was not sitting on, picked up the bike with his left hand and stuck it by the rear tire onto a large broken branch in the honey locust tree, all in one fluid motion. Raven did not even flinch; she had seen him do this many times before. The one thing that did baffle her was how the bike was never stolen. Jesse would just leave it hanging in the tree while they were on a date. Sometimes, they would catch people looking at it in wonderment.

Jesse jumped off the bench and faced Raven as she stood up. She was dressed for a warm summer day, in sandals, a white tank top and tight denim shorts, her long black hair flowing down over both sides of her shoulders. Jesse was a little tongue-tied and he couldn't think of a time she ever looked more stunning. He pulled her to him, looked into those emerald-green eyes and gave her a long kiss.

They sat back down on the bench to talk a little, since Lakeside didn't open for another thirty minutes.

"How's your mom doing, Jesse?"

"As sarcastic as ever. How are your parents?"

"As crazy as ever. My dad wants to put a spare toilet we have out in the front yard, with flowers in the top and bottom part of it. You can imagine how my mom feels about that idea."

Jesse was giggling. "I like the idea. It should be a big old sunflower."

Raven smiled and slapped Jesse's shoulder, "Don't give him that idea. He'll say things like 'Jesse said…'."

They decided that it was time to walk on over to the amusement park. One of the best things about Lakeside for Raven was that it was full of childhood memories. She grew up not far from there and her parents took her and her younger sister, Emily, quite frequently during the summer months. This amusement park also happened to be only six blocks south of the metal park bench she and Jesse would meet.

Just beyond the admission gates is the fried dough concession stand. This stand made donuts, elephant ears and funnel cakes, with all the different fruit and sugary toppings. Raven always liked to stop there and they would each get a fried treat and share a large ice-cold soda. They would find a shade tree with some grass under it and sit down to enjoy their spoils. While Jesse was chewing his chocolate-covered elephant ear, he saw Tommy Dubron and Sam Hart standing by the Cyclone roller coaster, buying some tickets. Both of them had a female companion. He watched as they stood around, waiting in line for their turn on the ride.

Raven finished her funnel cake with strawberry topping and threw the paper wrapper into the trash can. She rubbed her tummy, "Delicious!"

Jesse held out his hand and said to Raven, "C'mon, I see somebody I need to say 'Hi' to."

She grabbed his hand and walked with him. Raven finally saw what Jesse was looking at and a smile developed on her face.

Jesse approached Tommy and Sam and saw that Sam had a big patch on the back of his right shoulder. He figured that must be covering some road rash. It was taped on and there was a little blood to let everyone know it was a fresh wound. Sam was wearing a tank top, showing various other scrapes and visible bandages. The tank top probably helped; a sleeved shirt would chafe any injuries. Jesse let go of Raven's hand at that point. She stopped and stood back about fifteen feet.

He walked up and stood beside Sam for a few seconds, without recognition. Tiring of the wait, Jesse slapped Sam hard with an open hand on the right shoulder and joyfully said, "Hi Sam!"

Sam dropped to his knees in pain as he looked up at Jesse. "Ow. Dammit Jesse!"

"I owed you that one Sam."

Tommy and Sam heard Jesse's breathing and saw that intense glare in his eyes, just daring them to try something. Being sober and only numbering two, neither of them was in the mood for another confrontation with Jesse and they just nodded and looked back down at the ground.

Raven smiled then went over and grabbed Jesse's hand to lead him away. "You are so bad tonight." She heard their dates ask at the same time, "Who's that guy?"

They walked away, swinging their held hands, continuing deeper into the amusement park towards Raven's favorite ride, the Merry-Go-Round. Jesse never understood her fondness for this ride, but he endured it. The blaring music, dazzling lights and screaming of the patrons was not Jesse's preferred atmosphere.

Sometimes she would ride it five times in a row. Jesse would usually opt out on the third run, claiming dizziness.

Chapter Eight

Ryder came home from work at the local auto parts store in an unusually good mood. He called his family into the kitchen and told them that he had won a set of four Colorado Rockies tickets, the seats right behind home plate. Karen and Haylee were excited, but Gary acted like he didn't even hear what was going on. Ryder started to tell the story about how he won the tickets.

"There was this large clear jug of spark plugs and the person who wrote down a number on a piece of paper that was closest to the actual number of spark plugs won. There were a lot more in the jug than most people thought. Oh yeah, and your guess could not be higher than the actual number of spark plugs. I won it with a guess of 121."

Karen replied, "That's great, honey. When is the game?"

"It starts in about ninety minutes. I figured we could just grab some hot dogs and drinks at the ball park for dinner. Now go get ready, we need to be on the road within twenty minutes!"

Haylee turned and ran towards her bedroom in a cheerful mood. Karen set her beer down on the kitchen table and turned toward their bedroom. Gary remained seated at the kitchen table.

"Didn't you hear me, twenty minutes? Or do you not even want to go?" Ryder asked Gary.

Gary looked up and saw that same intense grimace on Ryder's face, which he always showed when they were alone. Gary knew his choices were to get beaten or go to the game and hope not to get beaten. He did know for sure that a refusal to join the family to the game would get him a beating. He kept his head down and replied, "I don't need anything else. I am ready to go when the girls get back."

"All right slugger, that's what I wanted to hear. This will be a grand old time."

Ryder turned to grab a couple of things he wanted to bring along. Gary just sighed and waited at the table for all of them to return. They generally left through the door off the kitchen if they were taking the car since it was next to the driveway. Within ten minutes, Haylee and Karen were back at the table. Ryder grabbed the keys. "Off to the ball park we go!"

The girls were in good spirits. Haylee was jabbering the whole drive to Coors Field and Karen was more coherent and engaged than normal. She was not as drunk as she usually was at this time of day. The traffic was pretty slow, due to the time of day and the extra capacity that the baseball game crowd was putting on the streets. They finally found a parking space that was under twenty dollars about eight blocks away from the field. Parking is expensive in Denver when the Rockies are playing and Ryder had a hard time paying more than twenty for a space. The Walker family joined the game crowd, walking as per the normal family hierarchy. Ryder was holding hands with Karen on his left and Haylee on the right. Gary was trailing along behind them a few steps, head down and hands in pockets.

Gary was not paying full attention and had fallen a little way behind the rest of the family. When Ryder got to the security admission gates, he looked around for Gary. He had all the tickets so Gary could not get in on his own. They were asked to step aside until their party was fully accounted for. Ryder was starting to get mad and Karen started frantically looking for Gary. She did not want this to get out of control.

She yelled, "Gary! Gary!"

"Right here, Ma." He quickened his pace and stepped up next to his mom. Gary looked over at Ryder, who was staring at him and shaking his head.

Ryder said, "OK, let's try this again. Come on, gang."

They all followed him into the game and found their seats. The set of four seats were great, right on the aisle and six rows behind the catcher. Haylee and Karen were tired from all of the walking and decided to stay at the seats and be waited on. They would guard the coats and seats. Ryder and Gary took their order, turned around and started jogging back up the stairs to the concession area. Ryder was behind Gary and when they had just left the girls' line of sight, Gary was taking a leap to the next stair when he felt something push the inside of his foot out to the right. This caused him to hit the top lip of the next stair with his shoe and stub his toe, but consequently he tripped and wiped out on the concrete steps. Luckily, he landed on his side and left shoulder, without banging his head. A couple of people saw it happen and were bending over to make sure he was all right, helping him up. Nobody saw that Ryder had caused the fall by sticking his foot in the middle of Gary's stride.

The two men helped Gary up by the inside of his shoulders and asked him again if he was ok.

Gary rubbed his shoulder. "I'm fine. Just a misstep." He looked back at Ryder.

Ryder said, "Well, let's get on with it, boy, before the game starts."

The two men looked at Ryder in a baffled way, but said nothing. Ryder was intimidating in person.

As they were walking up the last tier of stairs Gary heard in a very low voice behind him, "Maybe next time you won't mope along and make everyone else in your family wait at the security gate."

Gary was on the verge of crying. He could not believe how cruel this man was to him. What had he done to make Ryder so mad? He knew better than to show tears so he just kept his mouth shut and looked the other way until the episode passed.

Many times after they would get home from an outing that went sour, Ryder would leave Gary in the trunk for a couple of hours. He said it was to 'make the boy think about what he has done'.

Karen would start drinking the minute one of these incidents occurred. Nowadays, she kept a flask of vodka in her purse at all times. It was one of the cheaper Russian brands. Karen was not a connoisseur of vodka; she just used it for its medicinal purposes, to escape reality.

Haylee would just sit with her head down in the back seat and meekly cry on the way home. Once they got home, she would run to her bedroom then slam the door. She would spend hours crying and pacing in her room, trying to think of how she could fix her family. Haylee loved her daddy, but he sure was mean to Gary sometimes. He had never raised a fist or hurt her in any manner and she had never seen him hurt her mom, either.

After Gary was let out of the trunk, Haylee would hear him walk to the bedroom next to hers and shut the door. He rarely cried anymore, as if he had resigned himself to the fact that this was his life in hell. Haylee knocked twice on the wall that separated their rooms. If Gary knocked twice back that meant he was ok. Only one knock meant he was not. So far he had always knocked twice.

Diamond 24

Chapter Nine

Aaron Hardner, Jesse's father, had a few passions in life. One of them was fly fishing. He would disappear for a few days, sometimes a whole week, during the spring and fall, to pursuit trout in one of the many streams and rivers of Colorado. Jesse's boss, Mr. Roman, was a good friend of his father's and he would usually join Aaron on these fishing trips. They rarely brought any fish home; they liked to consider themselves catch-and-release fisherman. Aaron had taken Jesse a few times and Jesse truly loved it.

One evening while Jesse was lying awake on his bed, he was thinking about those times. He looked at the clock and it said 10:15 PM. Becky would be asleep so he would have to be quiet. Jesse got up and made his way through the house to the garage, as quiet as he could be. There were several boxes and some outdoor gear that they had kept after Aaron's passing. He rummaged around for a while then found back behind all of the boxes standing against the uninsulated garage frame two four-foot tubes covered with green nylon. He managed to pull them out after shifting some things around and unzipped the half-moon end on the one that he imagined would hold the fly reel. Jesse opened the other fly rod tube and discovered that both rods and reels were still there. A smile came across his face as he made a mental note to show them to Mr. Roman and ask him questions on how to get started.

He jumped a little and was startled by his mother's voice, "I was wondering when you would look for those."

Jesse knew his mom was a light sleeper, but he could not recall a single creak or thud that he had created while walking through the house to the garage. He turned to see Becky standing in the doorway leaning her shoulder against the wall, smiling at him.

"Your father always had big plans for you two to go on fishing trips, but he was always caught up in his work. He sure had a passion for it before he had to start making a living for a family. I know he is smiling down on you now."

"That sure would have been fun. Mr. Roman has mentioned some of the highlights on their fly fishing excursions. Peace, scenery, solidarity and stress reduction come to mind."

Jesse looked back down at the gear, then picked up and inspected a few of the fly rods. He noticed they were different weights and lengths. Some of the reels were lying unattached in a box. They too were different sizes and even the line thickness of each looked to differ. Examining one of the reels, he noticed there was a colored line underneath a length of clear line. He started pulling on one to get it out of the reel and noticed a few different knots tied along it, the line getting finer as it neared the end.

He muttered, "Man, I've got a lot to learn."

Becky smiled, "I'm sure you'll do just fine with a little instruction from Mr. Roman. In fact, he'd probably like to join you. I'm going back to bed now. Goodnight, Jesse."

"Goodnight, Ma."

Jesse reeled the line back onto the reel and placed it in the box. There was also a box that had some water sandals, high-top boots with felt on the bottom, and waders. Another box contained a net and a vest, and several clear boxes of different sizes and colors of flies.

He rummaged through a few more boxes that were next to the fishing supplies. In them were articles about great places to fish, when to fish them, and what to use. Several maps were printed out with written labels detailing name and locations, as well as the dates or time of year to fish a particular section. Yellow highlights outlined camping spots and fishing holes. All the information he needed to plan a trip.

Chapter Ten

Haylee had noticed that Gary seemed extra depressed while they were eating their breakfast: Fruit Loops in a bowl of milk and a banana. Gary had mentioned that he was going to ride the bus to school since it looked like it might rain. She decided she was going to ride with him and hopefully brighten up his day. This was not something new for Haylee; her mom could easily be on her second Bloody Mary or Mimosa by the time the school bus showed up out front.

Karen had no idea what Haylee does during the day. She herself was usually napping by 9:30 AM. This was not the way it was in the beginning. Karen was very active with Gary and Haylee for the first few years they were with Ryder. The early morning drinking started happening at the same time as the beatings. It was her way of coping with the abuse and dysfunction in the family.

When the driver stopped at the school, Haylee would get off and walk the one mile back home the way they had come. This time, though, she had a different plan in place. She knew that Gary's dad lived close to the school and she wanted to try and find him, to see if he could help stop the beatings. She had followed her mom a few times when she went to see Doug and she always met him at a bar about a half mile away from Gary's school. At least Karen would walk when she knew she would be drinking. She would go inside for a while and then come back out, usually with some money in hand. Haylee asked Gary about it once and he told her that she was probably collecting alimony money.

Haylee started walking further east, towards Federal Boulevard, in the direction her mom would stroll. She quickly realized that she had not paid enough attention to where her mom would actually go. It was hard to watch her mom and make sure she was hidden from her, as well as be engaged as to where they were headed. She thought surely she would recognize the building once she got to Federal. However, nothing looked familiar. It was very busy, with lots of road noise and honking. People were crowding the sidewalk and, being a six-year-old kid, she was not able to see very far in any direction.

A van pulled up next to her and a nice older gentleman stopped by the curb, "Hello, young lady. You look lost, can I help you?"

Innocent Haylee did not hesitate and blurted out, "I am looking for Doug. He is Gary's dad. Do you know where he is?"

Haylee noticed the man had a nice face with a large mustache and a big beaming smile. He had a plain blue ball cap that was covering his cropped hairstyle and he was wearing glasses. The man's arm dropped out of the van near her and she saw he had a bunch of tattoos. She took a step backwards as she sensed something sinister in his eyes.

"Where are your parents, darling?"

Right then she knew something was wrong with this man and decided to get out of there. She turned to run toward the back of the van but the side door opened up and she was yanked off her feet with a hand around her tummy and one covering her mouth, straight into the van. The side door slammed shut as the van took off.

***

Jesse had finished his route but had forgotten to leave one of his customers their carafe of grapefruit juice. He was back on the far east side of his route and decided to pull into the convenience store to fill his truck with gas for the next morning. He was talking with

Linda and noticed a young girl he thought he
had seen around the neighborhood before. She
was across the street and looking around like
she was confused. She had paced back and
forth three times along the same block of
Federal. A tan van with tinted windows pulled
up and stopped in front of the little girl,
blocking Jesse's view.

Jesse put his finger up and said, "One
minute, Linda." Then he ran out of the glass
entrance door to get a better view. He saw the
little girl start to run away from the van when a
large hand reached out and pulled her in. She
had let out a small scream that was stifled
immediately. He was in amazement that during
broad daylight hours nobody else had seen this
happen, or maybe people just chose to ignore it.

Linda came out, "What's going on, Jesse?"

"Call 9-1-1, Linda! Tan Van going south on
Federal! Kidnapping!" And Jesse was off,
running towards his truck. He jumped straight
up and into the driver's seat, released the brake
and fired up the truck. Before the van was out
of sight, he was racing down southbound
Federal Boulevard, in hot pursuit.

The driver of the van was obeying the
traffic rules, which Jesse figured meant he was
still unaware of his pursuer. As he got closer he
could not see through any of the windows of the
van; they were all tinted except for the
windshield. One window had a piece of

cardboard duct-taped over it. The van had no
markings and Jesse slowed a bit as he caught up
to it, to try and remain unnoticed. They were
approaching 80th Avenue, going south on
Federal Boulevard and the light was turning
red. At this point Federal is a three-lane street.
The tan van was in the slow lane on the far right
and the driver obeyed the signal, stopping at the
red light. Jesse pulled into the left lane next to
the van but there was another car in front of him
and he could not see any more of the driver or
inside the vehicle. He was looking into the
van's side-view mirror but again the windows
were tinted too dark.

The light turned green and the tan van took
off faster than the car in front of Jesse and kept
pulling further away. Its right blinker started
flashing, it was heading for the westbound US
36 highway on ramp. Jesse got over into the
slow lane and sped up to catch the van. There
was no erratic driving behavior yet, but Jesse
did not want this chase to get to the highway
where the speeds would be much higher and the
probability of people getting hurt or dead would
increase.

Jesse down-shifted the delivery truck and
slammed the gas pedal to the floor. The truck
lurched forward and was gaining quickly on the
van. When the RPMs were whining he shifted
back into fourth gear and was approaching the
left side of the van. The on ramp to the highway

was only a single lane so Jesse was using the shoulder. Finally seeming to notice the large brown delivery truck coming along the merge lane on the left side, the van driver started speeding up. Jesse just needed another ten feet and he could run them into the boggy grassy area where the van would surely get stuck. Jesse's delivery truck had just enough speed and once his front tires passed the front bumper of the van, he whipped the steering wheel abruptly to the right. The van's bumper collided with the tire and front bumper of the truck with a loud metal *crunch* that sent sparks flying into Jesse's open delivery door. It pushed the van sideways off the road to the right. Both vehicles rolled out into the grassy area and as the van slowed it bounced onto a grassy berm and became high-centered. The driver put the van in gear and punched it, then reversed and punched it, to no avail. The rear wheels were turning freely. Jesse stopped the truck, jumped out of the open door, running for the van. He pulled open the door of the driver, who was still concentrating on trying to get the van moving. It was an older man in the driver's seat but there was another younger, immensely overweight man in the back, holding Haylee. Her eyes were wide, pleading with Jesse for help. The younger man looked at Jesse and decided to let go of the kid and make a run for it. During that instant Jesse brought his right fist up, slugging the older man right between the eyes then grabbing him by his shirt collar and pulling him out of the truck onto the ground. The van driver lay limp and unconscious on the grass. Jesse saw Haylee still seated, shaking in the back of the van. He ran around to the other side.

"Wait right there!" Jesse turned and took off running after the other guy.

Little did the other perpetrator know that Jesse was a track star in high school. He kept looking back to see Jesse gaining on him at an alarming rate. He decided that his best chance of escape would be to knock this do-gooder out and then continue running. It took him a second to slow enough so that he could turn around to face his chaser. Just as he began to turn, his knees buckled and he went down hard, holding his knee, screaming in pain while rocking back and forth.

Jesse figured this guy wasn't going to get far. There was another hundred yards of open grass before he got to a large concrete wall. He stopped, turned around then jogged back to the van. By this time, there was a large crowd forming along the on ramp. Multiple police sirens were heading towards them from all different directions. Jesse looked at the van and saw little Haylee sitting right where he left her, wide-eyed and watchful. She had her hands in her lap and looked petrified, giving Jesse a small smile with a little wave as he approached.

"Hi, I'm Jesse. What's your name?"

"Haylee Walker."

"Hmmm, Walker. Do you live near 90th and Raleigh?"

"9034 Raleigh Street. I thought that was your truck. You look a whole lot bigger close up."

Three police cars pulled up and the officers were out and running toward them; some armed, others yelling.

Jesse held out his hand, "Come on Haylee, let's go talk to these folks."

They walked hand-in-hand around the van, back toward the crowd near the road. The policemen showed up and one knelt down in front of Haylee, "Hi. Is everything ok?"

She gripped Jesse's hand tighter, "Yes. Those bad guys tried to steal me."

She had turned to point at the van. The driver was starting to get up when one of the officers yelled at him to remain seated then proceeded towards him.

Another officer asked Jesse, "Who's the guy crawling towards the highway wall out there?"

Jesse smiled, "Not sure of his name, but he is the one that stole her." He used his fingers to double quote the word 'stole'.

The officer just shook his head, started walking after the obese guy crawling around in the field. Saying more to himself, "How come I always draw the short straw?"

Jesse blurted out, "You may need a forklift."

Chapter Eleven

A couple of detectives that Jesse had not met before pulled up to the scene in a dark blue sedan. They both approached Jesse and Haylee standing by the side of the road. Haylee was still holding Jesse's hand. One of the detectives was female and when she got close she knelt down in front of Haylee. Haylee was a brave girl and stood her ground.

The detective smiled, "Hi. My name is Detective Marilyn Schmidt. What is your name?"

Haylee took the proffered officers hand in hers. "Haylee Walker." Her left hand was still gripping Jesse's.

The other detective was looking over the scene and looked at Jesse, "Are you the one they are calling the hero on the police band?"

"Sorry, have never heard of that band before."

The detective developed a smirk then put out his hand to Jesse, "Detective Henry Wright."

"Jesse Hardner," he said, shaking the detective's hand.

"I am assuming that is the milk truck you were driving?"

"Yep."

"Do you mind walking over to retrieve your vehicle with me?"

"Not a bit." Jesse looked down at Haylee who was staring at him. "Everything is ok, these are the good guys. You will be safe with Detective Schmidt."

Haylee reluctantly let go of Jesse's hand then started walking with Schmidt towards the dark sedan. Jesse looked around for a minute, noticing the on ramp was still closed and there was an even larger crowd of people developing. Then a van pulled up to the ramp with a big satellite dish on it. In big red letters on the side it stated 'FOX 31 News'.

Schmidt asked Haylee, "Where are your parents, honey?"

"My dad is at work and my mom is at home drinking her special juice."

"What do you mean, 'special juice'?"

"That's what she calls it. She puts ice in a glass and then pours in some of the juice from the big glass bottle and mixes a can of pop on top with a spoon. It makes her happier. She will turn on the stereo and dance around the living room." Haylee paused, looking around at all the people staring and taking pictures then she continued, "Mommy usually gets tired then falls asleep after a couple of hours but she always leaves the stereo on. I turn it off so I can watch television. She is usually asleep before *Sesame Street* comes on."

Haylee would have just continued on and on, but the officer interrupted to ask, "Does your mommy know where you are or that you are missing?"

"I don't think so. I snuck out and rode the bus to school with my brother."

"Which school does your brother attend?"

"The big one."

"Do you know where you live, honey?"

"9034 Raleigh Street."

Detective Schmidt looked at a uniformed police officer who was standing near, listening to the conversation. "Can you do a welfare check and maybe bring her mom back?"

"On my way."

Henry asked Jesse, "Do you know Haylee?"

"Not personally. I have seen her in their front yard and they're on my delivery route."

"Anything unusual? Messy yard, beer bottles lying around, anything like that?"

Jesse developed a questioning furrowed brow. "Not that I've noticed."

Detective Wright looked him over, deciding he was not a threat. "I'll be frank with you,

Jesse. Haylee has not been reported missing yet and she has obviously been away from home, for at the minimum of one hour. We have a patrol heading to her house now for a welfare check."

Without saying a word to one another they turned and started walking back to Haylee and Detective Schmidt. Henry wanted to give his partner some alone time with Haylee. The moment they got there, Haylee grabbed Jesse's hand and stood next to him, facing the police officers.

Within three minutes their radios crackled. "Schmidt?"

"Here."

"I'm with the mother now. She was sleeping on the couch and she is quite frantic. She is grabbing her shoes and she will be riding with me."

"We'll be waiting."

The officer that had drawn the short straw was just now returning to the pavement with his cuffed suspect, who was sweating and breathing heavily. They'd had to stop and rest his swollen ankle several times making their way back across the field. Even though a heart attack may have been the correct sentence for this child abductor, it was against department policy.

A few moments later a police cruiser was working its way around the traffic jam. Karen jumped out the second the cruiser stopped at the scene and ran over to Haylee. Haylee dropped Jesse's hand and jumped into her mother's arms.

Detective Schmidt was glad to see this display of affection on both sides. She walked towards the pair, who were still hugging and now crying, too.

"Karen Walker, may I have a word with you in private?"

"Right now?"

"Yes ma'am, right now."

Karen looked up at the detective from her kneeling position, "Umm, sure. I'll be right back, sweetie, just wait right here."

Haylee stepped back over to stand by Jesse. She was looking intently in the direction of the detective and her mom. Jesse reached down to grab her hand again. Haylee looked up at him and smiled then looked back to her mom. While they were standing there Jesse surveyed the area, seeing a big red Dodge Ram pull up and park on the outskirts of the gathering. He'd recognize that truck anywhere, especially with the black bold letters on the sides; 'Romans' Dairy'. It would have taken Mr. Roman a few minutes to work his way through the crowd to where he stood. How did he know? Was he just driving by?

The two women looked to be in a difficult discussion. Mrs. Hamlin had her head down most of the time and was just nodding, as if she were a child being scolded by a parent. This went on for a while. Then Karen seemed to lift her head up and look at Detective Schmidt, wiping tears away.

"Look, Karen, I am a mother too. I get it. I understand sometimes you need to blow off some steam. From now on, make sure your child is in a protected state. I am not going to report this to child services but if I see Haylee outside, even in your front yard without supervision, she will be a ward of the state of Colorado and you will be up on charges for child neglect," Detective Schmidt looked Karen over then continued, "This is not a threat, this is a promise." Schmidt put her hand on Karen's shoulder and turned around with her to walk back to Haylee. Haylee again dropped Jesse's hand to run over to her mother.

Right then he heard in that familiar baritone, "Jesse."

"Hi, Mr. Roman. How did you know I was here?"

Mr. Roman kept looking at Jesse then nonchalantly pointed his index finger up. Jesse heard the helicopter now; he must have been too involved with what was happening to hear it before.

"Fran had the television on in the kitchen, as usual, and saw one of our trucks in that field. You were the only one that had not returned from this morning's deliveries yet," Mr. Roman said, looking around and back over at his truck then continuing, "So what is going on? The news coverage is vague to nonexistent. That policeman over there referred to you as a 'hero'." Mr. Roman used his fingers as quotes for the last word.

Jesse looked Mr. Roman in the eyes with a broadening smile. "Don't you believe him?"

Chapter Twelve

"It's a black Mamba!" Harry Hamlin yelled.

Terry Hamlin calmly replied, "Don't be silly. Those are in Africa. That was a garter snake."

The snake had crawled under an abandoned half-sheet of wood paneling which had been left in the open field. They quite often played and rode their bikes around in this field, just a block away from their home. On the far end of the field was a ditch that carried water most of the year. This was the reason that reptiles and small critters frequented the area. Turtles, frogs, raccoons, coyotes and of course snakes could be found here, amongst other critters.

Doug Hamlin bent down next to the paneling and picked up one edge to lift it high enough for them to look under. In the far dark corner a garter snake was curled up, trying to remain hidden. Harry reached in with his long stick and prodded the snake until it made a run for it off to one side. Once it cleared the sheet of paneling, Doug dropped the sheet and all three boys circled the snake until it stopped to coil up. Harry used his stick again to reach in and pin the snake's head down to the ground. Then using his other hand he grabbed the snake right behind the head and picked it up. The snake curled the rest of its body around his forearm and pooped all over it. A natural defense mechanism snakes use to try and get their captor to drop them.

Harry felt the smear on his arm, "Ewwww, gross. I hate that part about catching snakes."

Doug laughed and replied, "Yeah, but now you smell better than usual."

"Ass-face."

"You always have such descriptive phrases."

Terry intervened, "You two calm down. Now what are we going to do with the snake?"

"Let's just take it over to the ditch and let it go in the water. I like watching them swim," said Doug.

Terry turned sober and stared at Doug, "I say we kill it."

"Why? Then what do we do? Eat it?" Doug responded.

"What do you care?" Terry pressed.

"It's so unnecessary."

"Shut up, Doug," Terry snapped, and then turned to look at Harry, "It's Harry's snake, he caught it. Let him decide."

Harry looked up to see both of his brothers staring at him, in anticipation of his answer. He didn't want to kill it, but Terry was the oldest. He could also be very mean at times. Doug would always stand up to Terry; he was the strongest and he had the biggest heart, too.

"Come on Harry," Terry said, "Make up your frickin' mind."

"I, umm," mumbled Harry, "umm."

Doug tried to calm him down, "Don't be intimidated, Harry, do what you feel is right."

Harry looked meekly up at Doug and smiled a thanks. Then with fear in his eyes he turned to Terry, noticing he had that menacing smirk and was staring straight into Harry's eyes.

"I want to watch him swim, Terry."

Terry took a step towards Harry and Doug stepped in between them, to put his hand on Terry's chest.

"Not this time, Terry. You said it was his snake and he could make the decision. Let it be."

"You two are such pansies! I can't believe you guys are my half-brothers," Terry backed up and said, "Ok, let's do it then."

Doug looked down at Harry and noticed he was staring at him wide-eyed like a deer in headlights. He gave Harry a nod which made Harry smile.

Doug and Harry started walking in the direction of the ditch. Terry fell in beside them like nothing had happened. That was part of being brothers.

Terry, Doug and Harry Hamlin enjoyed catching the various critters in the field. One time they caught a rattle snake and took it home in a pillow case. It would not strike while it was in the pillow case, but if you tapped or shook the case in any manner the snake would start to rattle. They asked their mom to come outside and look at what they had caught. She looked at them with wary eyes but agreed to take a look. Terry was holding the pillow case. He grabbed the bottom of it, flipped it upside down and out dropped a four-foot Prairie rattle snake, onto the front lawn. Mrs. Hamlin screamed then jumped back up onto the porch, still screaming.

"What is wrong with you boys? That is a rattle snake!"

Terry giggled, "We know, Mom. Just thought you'd like to see it."

Harry said in glee, "Isn't it cool, Mom? Terry is good at catching it. Doug and I just watched."

"Not at all! And now that I know they exist around here we are moving," Mrs. Hamlin stated, and then she looked over at Doug, "Go get a shovel out of the garage. I want you to kill

it. We don't need any of those damn things
around here with all the kids and dogs."

Doug hated it, but he did as his mother
asked. Terry sat on the edge of the porch,
smiling at him while he had to go through the
motions of killing the rattle snake with the blade
of the shovel. Terry knew how much Doug
hated killing anything, even a spider. Doug
would catch spiders in the house with a jar, and
walk across the street to drop them in the field.

Later that evening the family sat down at
the dinner table for some of Mrs. Hamlin's
meatloaf with mashed potatoes covered in gravy
and a side of steamed green beans. Wanda was
a fantastic cook and the whole family always sat
at the table to enjoy dinner together. Nick
would turn off the television while they ate,
unless the Denver Broncos were playing at the
time. It was generally a jovial time with
everyone talking to each other, enjoying the
food. That night, the big talk had been about the
rattle snake. Harry was animated in telling the
story about how they saw the snake slithering
then it went under a rock. As they approached
the rock it had started rattling. It was loud and
fast and reminded them of a huge locust
buzzing. Doug bent down, struggling to move
the massive boulder, but after rocking it back
and forth for a time the rock finally relented and
rolled a few feet to the left. The snake was in
full view all coiled up. It struck out at them a

few times. Terry grabbed a stick and was able to pin the snake's head to the ground. They managed to carefully slide it into a pillow case that Harry had to run home to retrieve.

Nick sat there listening to the story, smiling and nodding. He had already heard from Wanda that the boys brought home a rattle snake. She was rather scared and curt with him when she called him at work about 'his boys'.

After the evening wound down and they were all turning into bed, Doug and Harry heard their dad walk down the hallway then open the door to enter Terry's room. Doug and Harry shared a room at the far end of the upstairs hall from Terry's. Their parents' bedroom, along with a bathroom was in between. They heard some voices and then a smack, and another smack. Then there was some sniveling and quiet crying coming from Terry's room. His door opened back up and they heard their dad walk back to his bedroom. He shut the door and everyone heard him say through the walls, "That damn boy isn't mine! Not sure what kind of trash you were dating before me, but it sure shows in the odd ball of the family."

Chapter Thirteen

John and Melissa had invited Jesse and Raven to join them on a weekend camping trip but Jesse and Raven had contacted a realtor to show them around a few homes on Sunday. They had decided to take their relationship to the next level and move in together. However, Becky needed or had become used to some daily help so it was not an easy subject for Jesse to bring up in her company. In fact, they hadn't yet, and Jesse was not looking forward to that day. Ideally, he would like to be within a couple of miles of his mother. Raven was not sure how her parents would receive the news, either. She did know her parents would first like her to finish school.

Nearly two years earlier, Raven had started taking nursing classes at one of those healthcare career schools that provided a fast-track towards a career and did not bother with the extracurricular courses. She was now at the point that she was a Licensed Practical Nurse and working at a local hospital. Raven enjoyed nursing and it made her feel good about herself; she was also making a decent wage with the promise of a better wage once she finished her courses and the allotted intern hours to become a Registered Nurse. Needless to say, she worked a lot of hours and since she was relatively new at the hospital, she was usually on the graveyard shifts.

Jesse had been saving money for years from his job at Romans' Dairy. A milk man's pay was quite a lot less than that of a nurse but that did not bother Jesse. Once he had finished his courses he had hopes of becoming an electrician. Jesse deferred to Mr. Roman as a confidant in his growing pains. He asked him for financial as well as relationship advice. Mr. Roman did tell Jesse that it was a good time to buy a home and that he would help with the down payment if needed.

This greatly reduced the burden for Jesse and Raven. They were worried about having house or car problems after they purchased a home and that their savings would then be depleted.

Each house they looked at, Jesse would be excited to see the garage and the kitchen, since he would be doing most of the cooking due to Raven's odd hours. Raven was more interested in the master bedroom and living room. They both agreed that a dog would be the first to join their family so the backyard needed to be of decent size to allow it to stretch its legs.

This was the first step towards their future together and they were excited as well as apprehensive. Neither of them had lived with anyone other than their respective families.

They met the realtor, Jane Finlay, at a coffee shop on Sunday morning. She had a list of ten homes that were within their price range and preferred location. They talked about each and looked at the different flyers and pictures online, which helped them to weed out four of them. That left them with six to walk through. They left Jesse's Firebird in the parking lot of the coffee shop and all piled into Jane's grey Lexus SUV. Realtors always needed to provide their clients with comfort and relaxation, to help ease their decision to purchase.

The first home, they didn't even go inside. It was next to a family who truly did not care for their yard or their cars. The whole front yard was two feet high with weeds, except for the areas where cars were parked, stifling the weeds from growing.

The second home was a nice bi-level but Jesse thought the garage was too small. There was no way a work bench would fit in the back of the garage with two cars pulled in and he needed work space.

The third and fourth homes had nice
garages but very small bedrooms and baths. It
was Raven's turn to say no. The next couple of
homes were also a no, due to the proximity of a
highway and the noise it distributed throughout
the area. Jane crossed off another home, stating
that the garage would not meet Jesse's
standards.

They decided on two more from the list to
look at and then call it a day. Jesse and Raven
did not want to spend their one day a week
together solely looking at homes.

As they pulled up at the next place, all of
them immediately knew Jesse was going to be
excited. It had a two-car garage with about an
eight- to ten-foot extension on one side. Jane
opened the garage with a code. Cupboards and
a work bench were already built along the rear
wall of the garage with a full-sized pickup
pulled in to one of the spaces. They entered the
home through a connecting door and Raven was
ecstatic about the deck off the master bedroom,
and the view of Mount Evans, as well as the rest
of the Front Range. The back yard was a tad
small but Jesse and Raven figured they would
be able to walk the dog around the elementary
school grounds across the street in the evenings.
Finally, Jane received a yes from both of them.

She took them out to lunch at a local family-
owned restaurant named Rosita's. The house
specialty was called a *Pablito*. A sopapilla

stuffed with your choice of meat then smothered with green chili and cheese. There were no leftovers when the waitress returned with doggy bags.

"I can see this table was hungry."

Jane said, "That was delicious. Thank you."

They started going through some of the paperwork. Jesse and Raven signed a contract to put in a bid on their first home. Both of them were excited; it was a big decision and they would be incurring a lot of debt, but they would be in it together.

As they were getting back into the Firebird, Raven said, "If both of my parents are home, let's tell them now."

"OK."

Carl, Ally and Emily Martin were sitting on the back patio under the awning, enjoying what looked to be lemonade. Rio was sleeping on the cool brick patio, under the table. As usual, the stereo was playing loud enough to be heard out back but not too loud to deafen one inside. Jesse followed Raven through the house to join the rest of her family.

"Here they are," said Carl.

Rio, who was deaf, felt the door open, looked around and jumped up when he saw Jesse. He barked once then ran over as Jesse knelt down to greet him. Rio loved when Jesse showed up; it usually meant some rough-housing and ball-throwing was in store.

Jesse said, "Hi, Mr. and Mrs. Martin."

They smiled and returned the 'Hi'.

Ally looked at Raven, "You look like you've got something to say."

"Jesse and I are going to move in together and we just put a bid in on a house," Raven blurted out quickly, sounding a little nervous.

Jesse's eyes grew wide; he smiled and kept playing with Rio. When the nervous Raven got into these types of situations, her approach was to just come clean.

Emily pumped her fist into the air, "Yes! It's about time!"

Ally was still looking at Raven in awe when Carl giggled and said, "I agree with Emily."

Raven still had her eyes locked on her mom's. "Mom?"

"I am a little disappointed, Raven," then she turned to look at Jesse, "and Jesse."

They were both taken by surprise with this response and remained silent.

She turned back to Raven with a smile, "Yeah, the whole moving in thing, which was expected and makes us all happy. But why wouldn't you want my advice on a home to choose?"

Jesse smiled and turned back around to throw the Frisbee for Rio again. This was Ally's normal wit.

Raven looked immensely relieved, smiled, and then hugged her mom. "You scared me there for a second."

"I know. The look on your face was priceless!"

Carl slapped the table. "Time to celebrate. I'll get a few beers for a toast."

Chapter Fourteen

Romans' Dairy was not a massive operation by today's standards. However, it did service a rather large area, which included the whole northwest suburban area of Denver Colorado. Mr. Roman had over 850 customers and employed nine delivery drivers. Along with the dairy business came the handling and care of a farm with its associated animals. On the Romans' Dairy menu of available items were goat's cheese, free range eggs, different fresh-squeezed juices and of course cow's milk, among other items. During the winter holidays they would expand their menu to include a few specialty options; eggnog, apple cider and homemade pumpkin pie.

In order to have these items available, the animals needed to be available too. For the dairy products, Mr. Roman had two dozen goats and 136 acres of cattle land. There was also an acre set aside for free range chickens, to produce the eggs. Recently, along the south side of the property, Mr. Roman had planted a two-acre orchard of apple, pear and cherry trees. The whole orchard was encompassed by grape vines white- and red- that were wrapped around four-foot trellises. Now there was only a need to purchase the citrus fruit products from another orchard since they do not grow well in the Denver area. Plus, these were the only juices and ciders Fran had time to squeeze into bottles or Mr. Roman would have to hire extra help and plant more fruit trees.

The Romans liked to keep the ranch fairly quaint; Jerry was dead-set on keeping it a family ranch and dairy. His brother Roger lived in one of the spare bedrooms in the upstairs of the main house. He was their only daily and constant ranch help. Roger, a decorated marine, came home from the Iraq war and with Jerry's help managed to get through a serious issue with PTSD. Jerry asked him to stay on to help out at the ranch. He would pay a fair wage, along with free room and board. Roger did like the quiet nature of the dairy farm so he was more than willing to accept this offer.

The Romans had one daughter, Jennifer, who was now attending Colorado State University, but she no longer lived full time at the ranch. She would come home most weekends to be with the family and her two daughters. Gabrielle and Shawna were the outcome of a high school relationship which did not last the course. Gabrielle, now eight years old, was old enough to help around the dairy farm with smaller tasks. Shawna was too young to be out and about on the farm so she stayed and helped Fran in the kitchen most of the time. The brightness of the young girls running around the old ranch gave it new life.

Once in a while, Mr. Roman would ask some of the delivery drivers if they wanted to make some extra cash to stick around after their delivery routes. He always paid a handsome wage for these extracurricular duties and would tell the drivers that the first five or six hands, or however many he needed, back to the dairy would be the ones to get the job. Mr. Roman always included Jesse in the fold unless Jesse opted out due to some scheduled conflict. Jesse had an extremely strong back, worked hard and was considered family by the Romans.

This job was going to take three afternoons with a crew of six, including Mr. Roman and Roger. They needed help with removing some old rusted water tanks from the cattle fields and then the placement of the new ones.

The first day they were out there with Mr. Romans' trucks and a few chain come-alongs pulling the tanks up onto flatbed trailers. Only two tanks would fit on a flatbed, partly due to weight restrictions but mostly because of the ten-foot diameter tanks. They were able to pull four tanks out at a time and then they would run them to the county landfill a few miles to the north and dispose of them.

The second day, they all climbed into Mr. Roman's two trucks and went to a nursery that also carried ranch and farm supplies. The nursery parking lot was nearly full of cars and people that were looking to expand their home gardens or plant flowers. With two big trucks towing twenty-foot-long flat-beds, they had to park on the outskirts of the lot. Shawna was feeling a bit cooped up so Fran suggested that she should tag along with Grandpa to the nursery.

Only two of the crew stayed back with the trucks while Mr. Roman, Roger, Jesse and the others went to look at their options. Mr. Roman carried Shawna across the parking lot then put her down once they got to the nursery entrance. She was being a four-year-old, running around, and looking at this and that. Jesse found an employee to ask where they kept the large water tanks. The three of them were talking amongst themselves to determine what size tanks and how many of them they needed. Mr. Roman asked if there was a bulk discount and the employee had to leave to go ask his boss.

Next to the water tanks and troughs were large mounds of loose dirt and piles of rock, of many different forms and colors. Between the large piles and the water tanks there was a huge scale that would weigh the dirt and rocks by the ton. A bobcat loader was used to load a truck that would then drive up on the scale to determine the fill-weight of the rock or dirt.

There were lots of people in the near vicinity. Some were looking at the different rocks; others at some of the water fountains which were near the water troughs. Jerry was talking to his crew and had his back to the scale. They all heard a little bit of giggling then a *'look at that toddler'*. That got their attention. As they were turning, in a very loud voice they heard Jerry's youngest granddaughter yell out to make sure that her grandpa could hear her. "Grandpa, look. I took a big poop!"

Jesse was the first to complete the turn and saw Shawna standing by the big rock scale, pointing to this little pile of something right in the middle of it. He started laughing wholeheartedly, as well as the rest of Jerry's crew, and the audience that had developed over the last fifteen minutes. Jerry looked down at his granddaughter and his face immediately started turning a bright crimson. It was hard to embarrass this man but Shawna sure had the knack for it. He was glad to see that she at least had her pants pulled up.

Mr. Roman started the process of walking down the high grass slope to his granddaughter. He was shaking his head and keeping his chin down. With leashed dogs being allowed on the nursery grounds, not far from the scale by the grassy area was a dog waste bag dispenser. He walked up, pulled one out and stepped onto the scale with his granddaughter running up next to him.

Shawna said, "That's a big one, huh Grandpa?" There was another rise of laughter from their audience.

Mr. Roman picked it up, then walked over to the trash can and threw it away. He reached down and grabbed Shawna's hand. "Come on up here with the rest of us, Shawna."

She skipped alongside her grandpa. As Mr. Roman approached his crew, all of them were tight-lipped and trying to remain serious. Once he got within talking distance Roger asked, "How much did it weigh?"

That set the whole crew off. None of them could hold their tight, serious faces any longer.

Chapter Fifteen

Ryder pulled up and parked in the rear of the
bowling alley, next to a big garbage dumpster
which blocked the only light. He had competed
in a Wednesday evening bowling league at an
alley near his home for the last few years.
Twelve different teams had signed up for it this
year. That was the most since he had joined.
His team was made up of three coworkers and
his neighbor Jack, who lived two doors west of
him. It was all men on the team and they
decided to call themselves the Auto Bachelors,
since most of them worked in an auto part store.
Jack was fine with it; he did not care about the
name, plus he was a bachelor. They would all
drink a few beers and razz each other with good
humor.

Once in a while, Karen would ask Ryder for
some alone time. She would make him take the
kids to the bowling alley on Wednesday

evenings so she could, in her own words, 'relax'. Ryder interpreted that word as 'get hammered'. As in most bowling alleys, there was a small arcade at one end that Gary would frequent when he was dragged along.

One reason Ryder liked to go to the bowling alley was the happy memories it brought back. His father took him bowling when he was younger; it was the only activity they ever did together.

His highest bowling score ever was 235. Now, he had just thrown a strike with his first ball in the tenth frame. If he could manage another strike or a spare, he could beat his own personal best. None of his teammates knew that Ryder's highest bowling score was at stake; he had not disclosed that information to anyone. They carried on with their gentle banter and sarcastic encouragement. He actually started to sweat a little bit and was zoning everyone and every distraction out, trying to keep his focus sharp.

His sparkly blue ball came up the ball return belt. He grabbed it with his towel and wiped it. Slowly, he turned and took the few steps over to where he placed his feet for his approach. With a deep breath, he settled into his lowered stance and tucked the ball into its holding pattern. Left, right, left … he approached then released the ball. His heart sunk a bit as he saw it land on the alley a couple of inches further to the left than he wanted. He stood still, watching intently. Ryder even leaned his torso a little to the right, thinking that he could somehow steer the ball.

The ball collided with the pins and after everything stopped spinning and tottering, there were two still standing. It was the nine and ten pin, both standing right next to each other in the far-right corner. Ryder looked up at his score and knew that he needed to pick up this spare in order to beat his high score. It had been since he was a young teenager that he rolled his best game. That was over twenty years ago, and he still had not managed to better that 235.

Ryder was still standing on the lane, staring at the two pins, when he heard his ball come up and get pushed out of the ball-return chute and clack against his teammate's balls. He turned around and once again grabbed his towel to pick up and wipe off the ball. His teammates were saying things to him but he just kept his head down to remain focused on the task at hand. Muttering to himself, "C'mon Ryder, two damn pins."

He stepped up onto the wooden-planked lane and positioned his feet where he always did on the far-right arrows. Confidence was with him, he had made this shot hundreds of times. He lowered his shoulders and tucked the ball into his arms. The only thing he could see were the two pins. He started his approach; left, right, left … his arm was starting to swing forward…

"Ahhhhhchhoooo!"

Ryder's arm flinched a bit and the ball flew out of his hand, landing straight in the gutter, next to his right foot. He watched the ball for a second and knew that his big game was gone. His shoulders visibly dropped and he turned around to look at his teammates.

"Bless you, Gary," said Jack his neighbor, handing Gary a tissue.

"Thanks," Gary reached for the tissue. He then looked over to see Ryder glaring at him from the bowling staging area. Jack also noticed the rather cold and icy glare.

"Nice game Ryder. You got a 229. That's the best game I've ever seen you bowl." Cody, one of Ryder's coworkers, said.

Another coworker patted him on the back as he stepped off the wooden lane, "Great game."

Jack piped up from the landing area above where the bowlers sat, "Congrats, Ryder, best game of the night."

Ryder just kind of acknowledged everyone nonchalantly and nodded his head to each. His smile was meager for the accomplishment and everyone figured he was just in one of his bad moods. Ryder was known to have some depressing moods at times but he had been in a rather chipper mood during the whole match until this last game.

Gary was wondering about the look his step-father had just given him. He was unaware of anything he had done to embarrass Ryder and sat down heavily in one of the many chairs that lined the landing. Haylee had seen the look too; she came running up to the landing and sat in the chair next to Gary. They were silent but both were concerned because Ryder was usually in a great mood at the bowling alley amongst his friends and had a few beers down the hatch.

The match ended a few minutes after Ryder finished. Jack was the last bowler on their team. The Auto Bachelors had won again and they were in second place in the league. All of the team members seemed happy and were congratulating each other; all except for Ryder. He was busy gathering his ball and changing his shoes. Once he had his bowling bag packed and loaded up he turned to his team and said, "Nice bowling, guys."

"Hey, aren't you gonna stick around and have a couple of beers with us like usual?" asked Cody.

"No, I'm not feeling well. I'll take a rain check," Ryder paused and looked over at Gary and Haylee, "Come on, kiddos."

Ryder gathered his stuff and started walking toward the exit doors. Haylee ran up and walked next to her dad while Gary reluctantly fell in behind at a slower shuffle, hands in pockets and head down. Jack was watching them leave the bowling alley. He felt that something just wasn't quite right. He thought about following them outside and seeing them off but decided it was all in his head and besides, Ryder was a good man. He turned back to the group and said, "This round is on me!"

"All right," Cody cheerfully replied.

The Walkers were heading around the building to the back lot where they had parked. Haylee was in constant chatter, asking her father questions about bowling and when she could join a league. She was trying to cheer him up. It was obvious Ryder was in a foul mood. That furrowed brow reformed itself and he was staring straight ahead with hollow eyes. His answers to Haylee were all one-word.

"When can I join a league, Daddy?"

"Soon."

"Can we stop for ice cream on the way home?"

"No."

"Do you guys always win?"

"No."

Gary wasn't listening to their conversation, he was wondering what was going to happen when they got to the car. With his stepfather's back to him, he thought about taking off and running across the fields and through the alleys to get home. He was trying to rationalize and determine if that would give Ryder time to cool down or if that would make him madder and he might lash out at his mom or sister. Gary kept wondering and rolling the evening's events through his mind. *What did I do to embarrass him?*

Ryder and Haylee reached the car. Ryder unlocked the doors and popped the trunk with his key fob. The second the trunk beeped and popped open, Haylee met her brother's eyes. There was fear and dread in hers while Gary's seemed to be full of anger mixed with acceptance. This was odd to Haylee; why wasn't Gary afraid?

Ryder walked up to the trunk and lifted it. Haylee and Gary stood still, staring at Ryder a good twenty feet back. He placed his two bowling bags into the trunk and then slammed the trunk closed.

He looked at both kids as he was getting ready to assume the driver's seat and asked, "What are you guys waiting for? Let's go."

Haylee's face grew a huge smile and she practically jumped into the passenger seat. Gary seemed confused, but also relieved. He stepped up and got into the back seat behind Ryder. Gary thought maybe he had misread the glare that Ryder had given him.

The ride home was full of more chatter from Haylee and one-word replies from Ryder. Her mood seemed to truly brighten once they were all in the car. Gary sat in the back seat silently and watched the suburban scenery scroll by. It was just a matter of a five-minute drive before they pulled into their driveway and came to a stop.

Ryder looked over at Haylee and said, "Last one inside has to wash the dishes for a week."

Haylee's door flew open and she jumped out, giggling, and started running towards the front door. She was already on the front porch, reaching for the screen door handle. Gary jumped out and started forward when his right foot kicked something in the driveway. He looked down as he was falling face-first to see Ryder's foot. He managed a glance at Ryder's face and saw that evil grimace before he hit the ground.

"Ooommmph."

Haylee heard the noise behind her just as the screen door was closing. She turned and looked out to see Gary on the ground with her father standing over him in a malevolent manner. Ryder's fists were closed and his shoulders were drawn tight.

Haylee screamed inside the house and covered her mouth in fear. She looked around the front room for her mom and saw she was passed out on the couch, her special juice bottle sitting on the coffee table. The stereo was playing some obnoxiously loud music but

Haylee decided to leave the music on in hopes of drowning out what was happening in the front yard. Unsure if she wanted to watch or if she wanted to hide and cry, she ran back and forth to the front room and then to the kitchen at the back of the house.

Ryder yelled, "You blew my highest damn score, Gary!"

Gary was face-down on the ground. He could feel the warm liquid seeping out of his chin and dripping onto the concrete. Gary did not want to stand up, he felt safer down there. He was still at a loss as to what he'd done to interrupt his stepfathers' game. He finally managed a meager, "I'm sorry."

Ryder was standing above him, his chest huffing and puffing. He was incredulous as to why this boy always wanted to belittle or embarrass him. It seemed to happen every time he went into public with this kid.

Ryder said, "Stand up."

Gary continued to lie on the ground. The warm liquid had now seeped further and was wetting his chest with warmth. He could not think of a way out of this situation.

Louder, Ryder repeated, "Stand up."

At this point Gary was visibly shaking. His knees were too weak to accomplish said task if he tried. In a small voice he wept out, "Please."

Ryder lifted his head back and laughed. Then he said, "*Please?* How about, please quit embarrassing me! You wimpy little shit," Ryder paused for a minute, waiting for Gary to reply, then he said, "I have tried to break that score for over twenty years and you blew it for me!"

Ryder had worked himself back into a rage. He reached down with one hand, grabbed Gary's right shoulder and flipped it up hard and quick. This literally picked Gary up and flipped him over onto his back. Then Ryder reached down with both hands and picked Gary straight off the ground by his middle biceps. He slammed Gary against the rear driver-side door, holding him there until he gained his footing and was standing on his own. Gary lifted his head to look at Ryder and to see what was happening. At that moment he saw Ryder's evil grimace and then a large fist was already in motion towards his face. He just watched Ryder's grimace turn into pure joy as his fist closed in and connected with Gary's nose. Gary felt the back of his head smash against the top of the car then bounce forward. His knees went numb and he felt himself dropping to the ground.

Ryder stood over him for a minute, looking down and shaking his head. He said something out loud but Gary could not hear him, with all the ringing in his head. He just lay there looking up at Ryder in a dazed and confused state, with a bloodied nose and chin.

Ryder lowered down on his haunches next to Gary and scooped him up like a bag of cement. He kicked his car door shut then carried Gary inside the house. Karen was passed out on the couch and Haylee was not around. Ryder carried the kid to his room and dropped him on his bed, then turned and slammed Gary's bedroom door shut as he left. Haylee's door was shut. He walked over, tapping lightly on it.

He heard a small voice say, "Yes."

"Everything ok, Pumpkin?"

That same voice replied, "Yes." Then he heard Haylee start to cry.

Once she heard her father go back to the front room, Haylee snuck out and ran into the bathroom. She wetted a wash cloth, grabbed a towel and went over to Gary's door. Not knowing what to expect, she slowly opened Gary's door to see him lying on his back in bed, touching the area around his right eye. She walked up to his bedside and made the universal sign to be silent, her index finger over her mouth. Then she cleaned up Gary's chin and nose with the wash cloth. He gave her a smile and gestured that she better go back to her room. Haylee leaned down and kissed his cheek then turned, exiting Gary's bedroom.

Haylee was in her room with the door locked, pacing around, listening to her favorite radio station, 98.5 KYGO, 'Denver's #1 for new country'. She was now past the crying stage and was in concerned mode. Gary needed help and she kept trying to think of who could provide it. She was not able to find Gary's dad. Then with the calmness of pacing finally came an idea and she blurted out to herself, "Jesse!" He had told her that day with the bad men that if she ever needed anything, all she had to do was ask.

She thought to herself, how could she get in touch with Jesse? Her parents would see or hear her if she got up early and waited for him in his delivery truck. She wasn't quite sure what time he showed up, anyhow. The pacing returned; back and forth across her small room. She would take twelve steps toward her closet, then a slight right turn and four steps toward her dresser, then an about-face and fourteen steps back to where she started. The whole time, she was thinking and had her head continually down, her hands behind her back.

Earl the elephant, the one that Gary had won at the carnival for her, was sitting in a small wooden rocking chair next to her dresser. The same chair used to hold her Cabbage Patch doll, but that doll was stuffed into the bottom of her closet, in favor of the elephant. Haylee would talk to the occupant of that chair while she was pacing around, trying to resolve a problem. She would nudge one of the chair feet as she walked by, to make the chair rock back and forth, which

made Earl seem more alive, like he was paying
attention to her.

Then it dawned on Haylee. *I don't know
where he lives, but I can write him a note and put it
in the milk box.* She started looking through her
desk, which was mostly filled with arts and
crafts supplies. In her bottom drawer she found
a box of Crayola crayons with some assorted
pieces of construction paper.

Chapter Sixteen

"Give me that John Elway!" Terry demanded.

"No way!" Harry replied.

"Look, you pipsqueak. I'm giving you a Bob Griese and a Bernie Kosar."

"I don't care. They are not Broncos and Elway was the best ever."

Terry vehemently stated, "Trade me the card or I'm gonna stick it where the sun doesn't shine and we'll see what it's worth then."

Terry did not realize that Doug had finished his business in the bathroom and was back in the room, standing directly behind him. He was trying to force Harry's hand to trade him the card while Doug was absent.

Doug said, "I got a foot I will stick in your sun doesn't shine and we'll see how that feels."

"Whatever, man. He never trades any cards and he gets all the good ones," said Terry sullenly.

The Hamlin brothers loved to collect and trade sports cards. They had baseball, basketball and football cards. At least once a week during the summer they would ride their bikes down to the local convenience store to buy a few packages of sports cards each. Harry loved the smell of the bubble gum that was wrapped inside each package. That smell would stick with the cards for a couple of months.

"Well, why don't we head on down to the gas station and grab a few packs and maybe your luck will change," replied Doug.

"All right! Let's go," said Harry.

Harry was more than happy to jump on the chance to go to the convenience store. It was a strict rule under Wanda and Nick Hamlin's roof that you must be thirteen years old to be able to leave the cul-de-sac without another person. Harry had a little longer to wait for that time so he was always in agreement when his brothers wanted to go explore.

While straddling his bike, Doug bent down, grabbed the rope attached to the handle and flung the garage door open. He waited for his brothers to exit the garage on their bikes as he did the same then to shut the door and locked it. The convenience store was six blocks away and it took hardly any time to get there.

As they pulled up to the store, the brothers had a habit of parking their bikes out of the way on the side of the building without any marked car spaces in the lot. This was where the store's dumpster also resided. Terry was the first one to pull up and hop off his bike. As he was pushing down the kickstand he noticed a drumstick lying on the ground next to his front tire. Neither of his two brothers saw him pick it up and slide it through the little metal rings that held his brake cables in place. He got it through two rings and it was nice and snug.

All three of them went straight to the aisle where the sport cards were sold in their mysterious packages. One never knew which players were represented in a package until it was opened. After they each picked a few they all milled around in the store for a few more minutes, looking at the various candy products. When each was satisfied, it was a matter of dropping their treasures on the counter and the cashier would ring them up.

Doug was the first out of the door. He went over and sat on the curb, in the shade next to the bikes, waiting for his brothers. He noticed something different about Terry's bike and walked over to have a look. Along the upper bike frame was a wooden drumstick wedged under the metal cable rings. *Where did he get that and why would he carry it around?*

Terry and Harry finally came out and it was decided that they would ride back and open their goodies in the cooler comforts of home. It was mid-summer in Westminster Colorado and the thermometer outside the store read ninety-three. They all hopped on their bikes and started the short ride home.

Doug was in front, his powerful legs pumping him up the hill. His two brothers were trailing behind. Harry was just slightly in front of Terry. This was by design of Terry. He pulled out the drumstick that he had weaved under the brake cable fastener. It was about as thick as a one-inch dowel. While Harry was paying attention to the hill and trying to race him to the top, Terry got a little closer without him realizing. When he was within reach, Terry jabbed the drumstick right into the spokes of Harry's rear tire then banked away to the right. The drumstick went a half-rotation in the spokes, until it hit the rear bike forks. The bike came to an abrupt screeching halt and sent Harry flying forward over the handlebars.

Doug heard behind him, "Arghhhhhh!" It was followed by a thump and then the sound of a bike falling to the ground. He had just crested the hill and he screeched to a stop and turned to look back down. He saw Terry still riding his bike up the hill and Harry in the street, trying to sit up and crying. He got to a sitting position and was holding his left knee, rocking back and forth.

Doug figured it was a minor crash and Harry was over-exaggerating the pain, since

Terry had left him on the ground. He was
waiting for Terry to crest the hill and pull up
next to him. As Terry got closer, he wasn't
slowing down; he went right by Doug without
even looking at him and continued on his
journey home.

Doug yelled, "Terry, what the hell, man?"

Terry returned to a sitting position so he
could let go of a handlebar then raised his
middle finger into the air as high as he could,
without looking back at Doug.

Doug was furious but he couldn't leave his
little brother alone in the street, injured. He
coasted back down to Harry, kneeling next to
him and noticing his left knee was scraped and
bleeding slightly. Harry had gotten over the
crying part, which was more due to the scare of
it all than any serious injury.

"Come on, Harry. You'll be all right."

He grabbed Harry's two outstretched hands
and pulled him up to his feet. Harry limped
slowly over to his bike, favoring his left knee.

"Hey Doug, something is wrong with my
rear tire."

Doug turned around, walked on down to
where Harry was standing near his bike then
noticed four of his spokes were bent way
backwards. The spokes were bent in the
opposite way that the tire would have been
rotating. He looked around on the ground and
there it was, about ten feet away from Harry's

bike. Doug walked over, picked up the drumstick and examined it closer. This was the exact drumstick that had been attached to Terry's bike.

"Harry, set your bike upright. I'll walk home with you. It's too unstable to ride like that but you can walk it home."

"OK, Doug, thanks," Harry feebly replied.

About halfway home, Doug asked, "Did you see Terry ride up behind you?"

"I just saw his shadow on the ground. He did get pretty close."

Chapter Seventeen

Jesse sat straight up, alarm blaring. It was Monday and the work week had just begun. Another warm day was in the forecast so he stuck with shorts. After getting dressed and pulling on his shoes he sat on the edge of the bed for a minute, gathering his thoughts. He stepped in the kitchen and made his mug of coffee to drink immediately, then another one for the thermos to drink on the delivery truck. While Jesse was drinking his first mug of coffee in the quiet confines of home, he would think about the things he needed and wanted to accomplish that day.

His thoughts kept coming back to Raven and how the two of them were going to move in together. That part was pleasant, but he still hadn't found the right words or time to talk to his mother about the move. He decided to ride his bike this morning. Maybe the cool air would help him with an epiphany. He stepped outside, reached behind the evergreen bush and pulled out his bike with his right hand. In his left hand he was holding a small backpack which he used to carry his thermos of coffee.

The moon was nearly full so he knew the predators would be out and about, looking for a meal. As he left the city lights and his tires dropped onto the gravel road he saw a few silhouettes of dogs running a little ways out in the field to the right. He knew where a den existed in that field on the upper side of an arroyo. He stopped for a second to watch and the largest of the three coyotes also came to a stop, watching him intently. This one did something truly out of the ordinary and peculiar. It sat down, staring at Jesse, pulled its ears back and raised its snout into the air. At first, Jesse thought it was just trying to catch a whiff of the air, but then the high-pitched howl reached him, with a series of yips that followed. Even though it gave him goosebumps, Jesse truly loved this melodic sound and sought it out whenever he could.

He arrived at Romans' Dairy, parking his bike near the front office, against the wooden split rail fence. Mr. Roman was in the office with his head down and a pen in his hand, looking at some papers.

Jesse lightly knocked on the office door as he was pushing it open. "Hi, Mr. Roman."

"Good morning, Jesse. Come on in and take a seat, I was just going over some of the maintenance schedules on the delivery trucks."

"Thanks. This is kind of hard for me, but you did say that you'd be willing to help Raven and I with the down payment on a home. I was hoping we could talk more about the particulars."

Mr. Roman's face grew a smile, "How did you convince that beautiful classy lady to date you in the first place? You should have sent her over to discuss the terms of a loan instead of your ugly mug. You probably would have gotten a better deal."

It was Jesse's turn to smile now, "Guess I should have taken a business course at the college."

Mr. Roman laughed then nodded his head, "Might not be a bad idea anyhow, especially if you are looking at buying a home."

"I'm worried the teacher wouldn't let me bring my pillow to class. Then I'd wake up drooling with flat hair from laying my head down on the desktop."

Mr. Roman laughed again and said, "Sounds about right. So I take it you two have found a home you agree on?"

"Yes, we have. It's only a mile south from Ma and not much further from Raven's parents.

The house is three beds and two baths and I believe the address is 8017 Raleigh Street. Just west of where 80th Avenue crosses the bridge that goes over Highway 36. It has a huge garage and a decent-sized yard, too."

Mr. Roman had never been known to beat around the bush, "That all sounds wonderful. How much?"

The directness didn't faze Jesse one bit, "They are asking 300. Raven and I put in a bid for 270."

"Whew, they sure want a pretty penny for a home anymore," Jerry paused rubbing his chin, then he continued, "What kind of down payment are you looking to do?"

"Twenty thousand."

"When do you need it?"

"They have twenty-four hours to accept or refuse our offer. I imagine it won't be for a while, I was more informing you of the amount and making sure it was acceptable."

"Ok, Jesse. You got my word. I will help you with the down payment once it's needed. We can work out a light payment plan."

"Thanks, Mr. Roman. You don't know how much I appreciate this."

"Of course, Jesse, don't mention it."

"Ok, well I better get to loading my truck. You know how Mr. Jones gets if his orange juice has not arrived by 7:20 AM."

"Be careful Jesse. Have a good morning. Glad to hear the news about you and Raven."

Jesse stepped out of the office, softly shut the door and jogged across the gravel lot to his truck. The loading only took about twenty minutes then he was off to start his delivery route. It was a good morning and he was lightheartedly happy and anxious to share the news with Raven. The route was moving along quickly, there were no new customers to search for hidden address numbers or find their hidden milk boxes. Some customers thought they were ugly so they would hide them behind a bush or a large planter.

Jesse looked into the milk box as he was placing an order in and noticed a bright yellow piece of paper on the bottom. It was that strong kind of paper that was used by kids to make crafts. He was just going to slide it to one side so the sweaty milk bottle would not ruin it when he saw his name written on the top right side of the paper. It looked like it was written in black crayon. He knew this was where Haylee lived and he figured she was just writing him a letter to say hi. After placing their full order in the milk box, he folded the piece of paper over twice, put it in his back pocket then jogged back to the truck.

He continued with his route, street to street, house to house; it was a typical delivery morning. After he filled the milk box on his last delivery it was 9:00 AM and he drove back to the dairy. Sitting next to his bike was the care basket with a little piece of paper wedged in, sticking up above the towel. He walked over and pulled out the piece of paper to look at it. It was one short sentence.

Jesse, I think I surprised Becky on the phone with talk of you two love birds buying a home. Sorry, Fran

Jesse mumbled to himself, "Oh man, I knew I should have talked to her earlier."

He stuffed the piece of paper back in the basket as he picked it up and straddled his bike at the same time. Fran was looking out the big kitchen window at him with a worried look while she was towel drying a big mixing bowl. He smiled and gave Fran a thumbs-up gesture. She smiled back and gave him a small wave, mouthing the word 'sorry'.

During the ride home he was practicing all of the things he could say to his mom. They were going to be close. He would come over to help her anytime she wanted. He would continue bringing over and cooking brunch each morning for them. She could set up his room as a recreation or sewing room; he would help her with that, too.

He pulled up into the driveway, hopped off his bike and picked it up to place it behind the evergreen bush. The van was in the driveway so he knew his mom was home. As he stepped onto the front porch he heard the television blare out, "Jimmy, come on down. You are the next contestant on *The Price is Right*." Despite being nervous about how his mom would receive the news, he smiled to himself and pushed the front door open.

"Good morning, Ma!"

"Good morning, Jesse."

Jesse decided there was no reason to beat around the bush; he was going to handle this as Raven would.

"Hey, Ma, Fran gave me a heads-up on how she spilled the beans," he paused for a second then continued when he saw he had her attention. "Look, Ma, we are going to be very close and…"

"Jesse, stop right there."

Jesse's heart skipped a beat and he was a startled by his mom's interruption. He looked closer to see that she was smiling.

"The only thing I have to say about the news is, it's about time! I am happy for you and Raven," Becky paused for a second keeping her eyes focused on Jesse, "However, I am not a fan of being left in the dark."

"Sorry, Ma. To tell you the truth, I was worried about how the news would be received and I have been thinking about how to break it to you for a few weeks."

"You don't need to think about the words to tell me, just say them."

"Ok, point taken."

"So where is this home you and Raven have decided upon?"

"8017 Raleigh Street. Less than a mile south."

"Delightful, I can't wait to see it."

"Thanks, Ma, I can't wait to show you. How about some brunch?"

"That sounds delightful, too," Becky smiled at Jesse then turned to look at the television and catch up on her game show.

In the kitchen, Jesse unraveled a scrumptious brunch that he figured Fran put together due to the recent events. Fran knew that Jesse liked to cook so once in a while she would put together a new basket with a recipe that she would wrap with the bread to keep it legible. Besides the carafe of orange juice, there were four fresh eggs, some thinly-sliced ham and turkey, a cheese he had not heard of named Gruyere, and several slices of marbled rye bread. There also looked to be a jar of raspberry jelly on the bottom. He found the recipe wrapped amongst the bread and when he unfolded the paper the title at the top read 'Monte Cristo'.

"Interesting... a French toast sandwich," he mumbled to himself, "I've never had one."

He layered them up as Fran instructed. A slice of bread, turkey, slice of cheese, then another slice of bread, ham, more cheese, and finally a slice of bread on top. After you whip the eggs with a fork, dip the sandwich into the scrambled egg mixture and fry in a pan on each side, including the ends, until the cheese is melted.

It was absolutely divine. Jesse had a new favorite sandwich. Becky enjoyed the Monte Cristo, but said it was a bit heavy for her and she preferred a runny yolk for brunch over a sandwich. Jesse thought, *I can't wait to make Raven one of these in our kitchen.*

Jesse sat down at the desk his father built for him and turned on the lamp that sat on the edge. He had started balancing his checkbook a few months ago, after he and Raven decided to move in together. He figured he should start being more responsible about keeping track of his finances. Calling the bank once a month wasn't Raven's idea of being financially responsible. When he sat down, he felt the note that he folded up and put in his back pocket earlier that morning. He reached back to pull it out and started unfolding it. His name was on the front and it was easy to tell that it had been written by a young child. When he got it fully opened he smoothed it out by rolling his forearm over it once.

'Jezee. My brothar needs help. Daddy keeps getting mad at him. Please help Gary, Jezee.'

Chapter Eighteen

Terry was bored of sitting on the couch with his brothers, playing Donkey Kong. They had been at this one video game for at least two hours. He started pacing around, thinking of something to do, and he found himself in the kitchen. A snack sounded good. Upon opening the refrigerator door, he noticed a jug of milk, some yogurts, the vegetable crisper was full and tonight's dinner was defrosting on the bottom shelf. On one of the door shelves sat eight beers.

Nick was at work and their mom was out back, tending to the garden. Terry looked out the back window to see her hard at work pulling weeds. He ran past his brothers, down the hall to Harry's bedroom, and yanked a case off one of his pillows. Jogging back to the kitchen, he took one more peek out the back window to see his mom in the same spot, then opened the refrigerator door. He pulled out all eight beers, stuffed them into the pillow case, then stepped into the front room.

"Come on, guys. Screw this game, let's go have some fun."

There was no argument from Harry or Doug as they dropped their controllers and turned off the television, following Terry out to the garage.

Doug noticed the pillow case and pointed at it, "What's in there?"

"You'll see."

Harry asked, "Where are we going?"

"How about the tree house?"

Doug nodded his agreement as they were straddling their bikes.

Harry said, "OK, but you guys have to help me get up into it."

It was only a three-minute bike ride to the tree house they had started building a few months ago from spare, unwanted parts they would find. Old pieces of plywood that were dumped in the field and boards that people would leave out by their trash cans. There was a spacious and surprisingly strong platform that rarely creaked, put together with plywood, but it had no roof yet. So they had to pick the non-cloudy days to go to the tree house. There were two sidewalls about six feet tall. The entrance was through a metal hinged lift-up trapdoor, which only had a rope for access. They were working on a ladder that would run up the trunk of the tree using wooden slats, but they had run out of screws to secure them.

Terry yelled down to Harry, "Just grab the damn rope, would you?"

"I can't do it. It's too hard, I can't do it," Harry was visibly shaking.

"Keep telling yourself that and you'll never do anything," Doug said as he climbed back down the rope to teach Harry, once again, how to climb a rope.

"OK, now squeeze your feet together and push up with your legs. Perfect ... now grab higher with your hands." Doug waited for Harry to finish that instruction, "Now, get a good grip with your hands then pull your feet up a little higher, keeping the rope between your feet." Another pause as he waited. "Good, see, you got it. Keep on going, I'll come up after you."

Harry's self-esteem boosted during those successful teaching moments. He always felt wimpy because he could not climb a rope, but that era was over. At the top, Terry actually grabbed his hand and helped him up through the door. Doug climbed through the opening in less than a minute after Harry.

Doug pointed at the case again, "So what you got there, Terry?"

Terry opened the sack and pulled out three beers, "I took Dad's beers. Thought we could have some fun."

Harry was astonished, "You are crazy! He's gonna be so mad. This will definitely get us the belt."

Doug said, "Hand me one." No sooner was the beer in his hand than the aluminum can top fizzed open with a *pop.*

Terry popped his too and raised it to Doug, "Cheers."

They both started drinking their beers. Harry had never seen his brothers get along so well. They were laughing and talking like he had never seen. Terry even stood up and walked over to sit closer to Doug. Harry decided if this stuff made everyone get along, it couldn't be that bad, and he reached over to grab his beer. He was still reluctant to try it, but one more look at his brothers convinced him.

Harry took a big swig and immediately spit it up onto the floor, "Oh gross, that tastes like crap!"

Terry got on him, "Hey, quit wasting the beer. If you don't like it, don't drink it."

"That was my first taste of beer. Do you guys really like this stuff?"

Doug replied, "After the first one they get better."

Harry asked, "How do you know?"

"I've taken beers out of the refrigerator before, just not eight of them all at once. You can take one or two, sometimes even three, and Dad never notices," Doug started laughing, Terry joined in.

Terry slapped Doug's shoulder, "You dog."

Harry was completely flabbergasted by this revelation. The things his brothers must do without his knowledge. He tried another drink and made himself keep it down this time. After quite a few more sips, thirty minutes had passed; he was feeling lighter and giddy. Harry was really enjoying the moment, his brothers were being open and candid and there was none of the usual tension in the air.

He stood up, "I have to pee."

"Go stand in that corner without the wall and pee over the side," Doug instructed.

"What if somebody sees me?"

Terry laughed, "Then pee on them and flip them the bird."

Doug started laughing harder, "What is there to see?"

This got both of his big brothers rolling around on the floor of the tree house. Harry counted seven empty beer cans including his. He opened the pillow case, saw that there was one left, and popped the top.

"Hold up there, twerp," Doug said, "We're going to share that last one."

They passed it around twice then it was back to Doug's hand. He tossed his head back and drank the rest of the last beer, which was over half-full. Neither Terry nor Harry complained, they were having too much fun to ruin it with squabbling.

An hour passed by, they were starting to get tired and coming down from their high.

Terry blurted out, "You guys want to get some more beer?"

Doug replied, "Of course, but what are you thinking?"

"Maybe from the store about a mile away, the one with the big neon sign that says 'Liquor' on it? Sometimes there is a bum that hangs out in the back you can give money to and he'll bring you back what you order."

"Worth a try," Doug replied.

Terry shimmied down the rope first, then Doug, with Harry right above him. He was worried that in his drunken state, Harry would lose his grip and slide down to the bottom too fast and hurt himself. Amazingly, they all managed to descend from the treehouse successfully. They pulled their bikes from the tall grass that lined the base of the tree and headed for the rear of the liquor store.

Doug was the first on the scene, "There is no bum back here, Terry."

"Dang, OK, let's split up and ride around for a closer look. Sometimes he is behind one of the other stores or in that line of trees across the street."

Doug replied, "I'll take the trees."

Harry decided, "I'll go this way."

"I'll go the other way. Let's meet back here in ten minutes," instructed Terry.

They all met back up with negative news on the bum's location. Doug and Harry had admitted defeat and were ready to go back home.

Terry was not giving up hope, "There is still a way."

Doug asked, "How is that?"

"Follow my lead. You two guys go hang out by the cooler with the sodas."

"And where are they? I've never been in this store," Doug asked.

Harry said, "Yeah, me neither."

"Right up front, to the left of the cash register."

The three of them walked in single file. Terry asked the store clerk, "Can I use the restroom?"

From behind the counter, the clerk answered as he pointed, "Sure. Back corner on the right."

"Thanks," Terry headed toward the restroom. Doug noticed that the restrooms were next to the beer coolers. He and Harry stood by the soda cooler and were looking at their different options. The store clerk paid them no mind and sat down on his stool to resume his crossword puzzle.

Doug heard the restroom door open back up and saw the top of one of the glass cooler doors open, then shut. Terry came around the far side of the aisles so the clerk could not see what he was carrying. Once he got to where Doug and Harry were standing, the store clerk looked up and Terry took off, running right through the exit door.

Doug muttered, "Damnit," and was right on Terry's tail. Harry fell in behind, but was too slow off the mark.

The store clerk managed to grab Harry by his right shoulder and the nape of his neck. Doug stopped to look back and see Harry in the clerks grasp. Harry's eyes were pleading for help. Doug mouthed 'sorry' then turned and followed Terry for their bikes. Terry pulled out the pillow case as he was running and dropped the six-pack of beer into it. They were on their bikes, heading back to the treehouse.

Gasping for breath, Doug said, "Damnit, Harry got caught."

"I saw. Guess there will be hell to pay when we get back home."

That took some of the wind out of their sails as they pulled up to the treehouse and silently went through the motions of climbing the rope ladder. Terry carried up the pillow case clenched in his teeth. He and Doug resumed their fun shortly after they cracked their first beers and saluted Harry. After a couple of hours, they decided to head home. As they rounded the corner to their street they saw a police car in the driveway.

"Let's go back to the treehouse for an hour," Terry said.

Doug agreed, he did not want to speak with the police. They ended up falling asleep for two hours in the tree house. Terry was using the pillow case for head support; Doug just used his arm. It was starting to get dark when Terry shook Doug awake.

The police car was gone when they pulled into the driveway. As they squeaked open the front door, Harry was sitting on the couch in tears. Nick heard the boys right away, grabbed his keys, shouldered Doug to the side to get at Terry and ushered him right back outside. Doug stood there, stunned. They all heard some yelling outside, along with a couple of audible smacks, then the trunk lid was slammed shut.

Nick came back inside alone, shouldering past Doug, who had remained in the same spot awaiting his punishment, walked back over and sat on the couch to continue watching the Rockies game.

"You know what you did wrong, Doug?"

"Yes sir."

Nick turned to look at Doug, "Good. Do not follow Terry's lead anymore; think for you and your brother," he turned back to the television, "now get over here and watch the rest of the game with us."

Everyone was silent and visibly scared, except for Nick. "You guys are lucky that the store owner is not going to press charges. He just wants restitution." The silence resumed for a couple more minutes.

He looked at Doug again, "You know what really chaps my ass? That little bastard didn't even leave me a single beer for after work!"

Chapter Nineteen

Halfway through his route, Jesse's phone started ringing. He pulled to the side, stopped, and noticed it was Raven calling, "Hey, babe."

"Good morning, Jesse. I feel awful, as you know my parents are out of town and I forgot Emily's birthday."

"When was it?"

"Today."

"Then you haven't forgotten it. Tell her I will be picking everyone up at 6:00 PM."

"You are the coolest. Love ya, bye."

Jesse looked down at his phone; Raven had hung up before he could say anything more. Like where they were going. She always did like spontaneity. Maybe that was her way to enforce it; just not ask. He put the phone away and continued his route. While driving around this morning, he had heard on the radio that one of his favorite local blues rock bands was playing at the Buffalo Rose in Golden Colorado tonight. He was sure that his two dates would enjoy the band, too.

Jesse had just completed his route. He looked down at his gas gauge and realized he had forgotten to fill up. The gauge was near empty. "Damnit!" Without delay, he turned around to make a bee line for the gas station, hoping he had enough fuel.

Linda was still manning the convenience store.

Jesse stepped in, "Good morning, Linda."

"Jesse, I haven't seen you since that ungodly incident you were involved in," Linda paused. "How is the little girl?"

"She's fine and so am I."

"I didn't ask about you. So that's it, nothing more for the gossip tree."

He laughed, "I'm sure you'll think of something, Linda. Pump seven, please."

"You got it. Take care, Jesse."

Pulling into Romans' Dairy gravel parking lot, he spotted the care basket in its usual spot next to his bike in the shade. He had been hungry all morning and seeing the basket made his tummy growl. After he was done putting away his leftover items in the cooler, he started for his bike. Fran was in the kitchen with her granddaughters, Roger was working on some fencing around the chicken coop, and Mr. Roman was on the phone in his office. He waved at each, received a wave from each in return, then jumped on his bike and had to endure the most delightful smelling basket all the way home.

He smiled as he was opening the door and heard, "Jamey Perry, come on down, you are the next contestant on *The Price is Right*!" He thought, *It's all about the timing.*

"Good morning, Ma."

"Good morning, Jesse. Look at this guy. He just bid $1200 on a food processor."

Jesse had no idea how much a food processor cost, "I'm not sure what Fran made for us today, but it smells wonderful. I'm heading for the kitchen."

Under the cotton cloth, the first item revealed was a carafe of orange juice, then there was a flask of maple syrup and on the bottom, wrapped in parchment paper, what looked like four corn dogs. He pulled out one of them to inspect it a little closer. There was a sticky note from Fran that said to reheat the syrup and the dogs in an oven at a low heat for thirty minutes. Underneath, the instructions it said '*bacon wrapped pancake battered breakfast sausage links*'. Upon reading this, he nearly started slobbering like a hound dog.

Jesse brought his mom's plate out with a glass of orange juice and a dipping bowl of warm syrup. When he set it down in front of

Becky, she looked up at him with a curious glance, "Corn dogs with syrup?"

"Try one."

They sat at the little kitchen table. It was in the perfect spot for Becky to view her game shows on the television. Becky was humming lightly while she was chewing. This meant that she was enjoying her meal.

Jesse's phone rang. He stood up and went back to the kitchen so he wouldn't talk over Drew Carey, "Hello."

"Hi, Jesse, this is Jane Finlay."

"Hi, Jane."

"Good news, Jesse. Your offer was accepted by the owners."

Jesse excitedly said, "All right!"

"Listen, I have to go, just wanted you to know. I'll be in touch."

"Thanks, Jane."

Becky had actually turned away from the television during *The Price is Right* and was looking at Jesse in anticipation.

"Well Ma, you are the first to know that they have accepted our offer on the house."

"Oh, Jesse, that is wonderful. I am so happy for you and Raven. Now, I must go call Fran."

Jesse started the Firebird, drove to the Martins' home, pulled up next to the sidewalk and honked the horn. He figured since her parents weren't home, there was no need to go inside to say hello. As they came out the door, Jesse noticed there is a third figure and it was a male. Raven was the first to the car; "Emily invited her boyfriend, Paul, to go. Hope that's OK?"

"Of course it is, jump on in, Paul."

As Emily and Paul started to crawl into the back seat, Paul held out his hand to shake. "Hi, Jesse. Glad to finally meet you."

Jesse shook his hand, "Likewise."

Raven dropped in on the passenger seat, "So where are we going?"

"Well, I have some stuff in the trunk I want to drop off at the dump, then there is a new book out I want to see if the library has in stock."

Emily asks sarcastically, "Have you ever been in a library, Jesse?"

Raven laughs, "Hell, he doesn't even know where one is."

Jesse replies, "I do too, that's where I used to meet my previous girlfriend."

Raven just smiled and smacked his shoulder, "OK, wiseass, then lead on."

He looked in the rearview mirror to see Paul smiling. *This kid seems all right; firm handshake, too.*

They found a spot to park a few blocks away from the Buffalo Rose. The town was packed, as usual.

Jesse turned off the car. "OK, my plan, there is a great local blues rock band playing at the Buffalo Rose tonight that starts in an hour, which gives us just enough time to get a few slices at Woody's Wood Fired Pizza."

Emily replied, "Yes! This is great! Thanks, Jesse and Raven."

The four of them ended up playing a couple games of pool while eating their dinner. Emily and Paul won both games. Paul was very good and made it a point to call each shot. They walked the necessary block-and-a-half to the north and bought their general admission tickets to the concert. By the time the band was done it was near 10:00 PM and they made their way home.

Emily unlocked the front door and Paul followed. Raven had bought an ice cream cake earlier and Emily could not wait to cut into it.

Jesse grabbed Raven's hand, "Let them go. How about you and I hang out on the front porch swing for a few and enjoy this beautiful starry night?"

Raven smiled, "I'd love to."

Emily yelled from the kitchen, "We're not waiting for you guys."

Raven laughed and looked at Jesse, "She loves ice cream cake." She leaned

forward to claim a kiss and Jesse obliged.
"Thank you, Jesse. That was a great time and
you really helped me out with Emily. She will
talk about this night for a while."

"I hope she enjoyed it. I think she found a
great guy there, too."

"They do seem to mesh well. I fear she has
fallen for him already, after only a couple
months. That must run in the family."

"So I have this dilemma, I was hoping you
could help me with."

"Sure, what's up?"

"I got another note in a milk box a couple
days ago." Raven's face fell, remembering the
last time Jesse had found a note in a milk box;
and all the trouble which that note had brought.
Jesse reached into his back pocket and unfolded
the piece of paper, "Check this one out."

"Looks like a little kid wrote it."

"She did. Her name is Haylee Walker.
She's the one that was kidnapped, when I
happened to be in the right spot at the right
time."

"Are you kidding? The truth is stranger
than fiction," Raven said as she was thinking.
"Hmmm, have you talked to her about this?"

"Nope. I don't know how to approach her,
or the situation. Wouldn't it look weird if I just
showed up and wanted to talk to Haylee?"

"Probably not, you big lug, since you pretty
much saved her life. But if you must, forget an

item on their delivery and take it back later when they are awake."

"That's a great idea. I knew you'd figure a way."

"I'm sure it's nothing. Or maybe, just maybe, she has a crush on this hunk of a man," Raven said, pinching his cheek and stealing another kiss.

Jesse smiled and then it dawned on him. "Oh hey, I almost forgot. They accepted our offer on the house."

Raven jumped up. "Sweet!" Then she slapped his shoulder hard, "Damnit, you have been keeping that from me all night!"

Chapter Twenty

"Hi, Mrs. Wright. This is Karen Walker and I have to tell you. Gary has caught an awful cold," Karen stopped and listened for a moment, "Yes. He has a fever and a heavy cough. I am going to have to keep him out of school until this clears up." She listened again. "Well, thanks Mrs. Wright, I will let him know. Have a good day."

Ryder had been getting more careless and increasingly aggressive with Gary lately. There was no way Karen could hide the damage done to Gary's face and arms this time. She tried a different rouge but the one with the best color match was easily identifiable as makeup when applied, which may cause some of Gary's classmates to challenge him.

Karen decided it was best to keep him out of school for a few days until he had healed enough. This also meant that he could not be

going outside, where others would see him.
She went to a discount store, bought Gary
some new comic books and a new video
game he had been requesting, all to try and
keep him from becoming too bored inside
and sneaking out.

After she returned from the store, it
took Gary less than five minutes to
commandeer the television so he could
hook up his game console. He was excited
to play this new game; Jeremy had been
talking it up for a few weeks already, so he
knew he had some catching up to do. As
far as Jeremy knew, Gary had never played
the game before. Gary wanted to keep it
that way so he could shock Jeremy with his
game play next time they were at his
friend's house.

Karen was in the kitchen with some
music playing lightly. Since she was losing
the television for the day, maybe even
longer, she decided to make some meals for
the week and surprise her family. It had
been a while since the family had sat at the
dinner table together. Through the kitchen
window she could see Haylee in the
backyard, swinging on her two-passenger
lawn swing with Earl the pink elephant
sitting across from her.

While she was out shopping for Gary,
she had also stopped at the grocery store

and picked up the ingredients for the meals she planned to prepare. She looked in the refrigerator and noticed there was no milk, which was needed for her homemade macaroni and cheese. Lately, Haylee had been retrieving the items from the milk box. Karen went to the front porch to see if Haylee had forgotten this morning but there was nothing in the milk box.

"Shoot. Gary, I need to run back out and grab some things at the store."

"OK, Mom."

Just as she had grabbed her keys and purse, the doorbell rang.

Karen looked through the peep hole and saw a Romans' Dairy delivery truck parked out front. She pulled the door open and the young man that had saved her daughter was standing there, holding a carton of eggs and a bottle of milk.

"Hi, Mrs. Walker, I'm sorry these are late but I forgot them this morning."

"Oh great, I was just heading out to buy some."

"I'm glad I caught you first. Again, I'm sorry."

"No worries; sorry, I am bad with names. Is it Jason?"

"Close, it's Jesse," Jesse stuck out his free right hand to shake Karen's.

"I'm sorry, Jesse. Jesus, I should remember your name after last week."

"That's OK, Mrs. Walker. Is Haylee around?" Jesse noticed how Mrs. Walker sure looked a lot better than she had that fateful day. Her eyes were clear and hair was brushed.

"Please call me Karen," she smiled, "Yes. She is out back playing on her jungle gym playhouse thingy."

"May I speak with her?"

"Of course, c'mon inside, Jesse."

Jesse stepped inside, looking around and saw a young male teenager returning his gaze. The teenager was holding a game controller, sitting in front of the television. His black eye was unmistakable. There was also a gash on his chin and a scrape on his left cheek, with various small scratches up and down his forearms. He went back to the television.

Jesse held up his hands, "Karen, would you like me to put these in your fridge?"

"Oh sorry, Jesse, let me take those. Can I get you something to drink? Glass of water?"

He looked over Karen's shoulder through the kitchen window and saw Haylee through an open door, playing with a couple of dolls in a little wooden cottage. It was no bigger than a kitchen pantry, but he could see the enticing aspect of a remote retreat where you were the queen. There were some chairs around the table, which each held a doll with a tea cup in front of them. "Sure, I'll take a glass of water. Thanks."

Karen looked out the window as she was filling the glass with water, to see what Jesse was so interested in. "Haylee really enjoys her little cottage. She is always asking to sleep out there, but her dad won't allow it. He says there are coyotes and crazies around here and that we all need to sleep indoors to stay safe."

"I have seen some coyotes around here, Karen," Jesse heard the game stop and knew the teenager had looked over at him again. "Mind if I step outside and talk to Haylee. I haven't seen her since the kidnapping episode. How is she holding up?"

She handed him a glass of ice water, "She's a stronger girl than I am. Now get out there, she is always talking about you and will be happy to see you."

He opened the screen and took one step out, "Jesse!" Haylee was running his way. She had her arms spread wide, as if hugging an old-time friend, and jumped into his hands. Jesse set his glass on the railing just in time to catch her, picking her up and looking back at the kitchen window to see Karen smiling at them. Caught off-guard by his reception, he thought, *A little odd for someone they barely know.*

Jesse set the girl back down on the ground and they slowly wandered toward the cottage.

Haylee looked up at him with a big smile, "I knew you'd come." She was quiet for a second then asked, "Did you find my letter in the milk box?"

"I did, that is why I am here. Does anybody else know about the note?"

"No way! I'd get into trouble."

"Is that your brother playing video games in the house?"

"Yes."

"How'd he get the black eye and scratches?"

Haylee looked down and in a saddened voice, "Sometimes Daddy gets mad. He doesn't mean it."

"Does your mommy know?"

"Yes, she just cries then drinks her special juice and sleeps on the couch."

They both lifted their heads in the direction of the garage when they heard a car pull up and screech to a halt. Karen was no longer in the kitchen window. A screen door squeaked open then slammed shut. All of the noises from within the home, including the video game, were audible in the backyard since every window was open.

A male voice filled the house. "Hey babe," then a short pause, "now where's my little girl?"

Haylee turned on the dime, running to the house and yelling, "Daddy!"

Ryder appeared at the back screen door, opening it to see Jesse standing by the wooden cottage he had built for Haylee.

"Who the hell are you?"   Ryder stated as he aggressively barreled out the screen door in Jesse's direction, not taking his eyes from Jesse. Without slowing, Ryder reached over the white picket garden fence, grabbing a spade fork that had been stuck in the ground since spring and had developed rusty tips. Jesse turned half to the side, readied his feet and got into his Kung Fu fighting stance.

Karen appeared at the back screen, screaming, "No, Ryder! That's the boy who saved Haylee. He just stopped by to say hi."

Ryder slowed, still holding but lowering the spade fork. He walked right up to Jesse, who had retaken a normal stance. They sized each other up as two alpha males would. Ryder was only an inch taller but outweighed Jesse by thirty pounds and had a strong air of confidence.

Ryder broke the silence. "Karen tells me you're our paper boy or something?"

"I believe you'd call me the milk man."

Chapter Twenty-One

"I don't care if your bike has a flat tire! Get to walking or go grab your skateboard, nimrod," Terry yelled at Harry then smacked him upside his head by the ear.

Doug asked in repulsion, "Hey man, why do you have to be so hard on him?"

"Look, he needs to quit being such a nerd or he is gonna get his ass kicked all the way through middle and high school."

"Whatever, man. Lighten up or I'll smack you upside the head."

Terry pushed out his chest and strutted closer to Doug, "Wanna try that right now?"

Doug was sitting on his bike. He stood up and dropped his bike to the right, "Be careful what you ask for."

Terry was faster than Doug, but not stronger. He brought his right fist back,

swung at Doug and connected with his left
cheek. Doug's head dipped to the right for a
second and then snapped back. It did not slow
down Doug's steady progress toward Terry.
Harry turned around just in time to see the
punch. He watched the fight intently. Terry
reared back his right arm again and threw his
fist at Doug. The second he did, Terry knew it
was the wrong move. Doug grabbed his fist in
mid-flight with his left hand, reached out with
his right hand, and wrapped his fingers around
Terry's throat. Doug kept the march going all
the way to the garage wall and pinned Terry
against it. Terry was gasping and trying to free
himself from Doug's grip, with no success. He
was hitting and pushing Doug with his left
hand, but that too had no effect.

Doug was looking into Terry's eyes. "You
finished yet?"

All Terry could do was squeak out what
sounded like a hiss. He tried again and this time
it had a little more structure to it, coming as a
hoarse, "Yes."

Doug relented and dropped his arms. Terry
thought about punching him in the face again,
but he decided this was not the right place or
time. Harry developed a little smirk. There was
security in knowing his big brother could wipe
the floor with Terry's face.

Terry bent over and in a raspy voice said,
"Jesus, Doug. Are you trying to kill me?"

Doug turned and walked back to pick up his bike and nonchalantly replied, "Maybe."

It was quiet for a minute in the garage. Terry was regaining his composure and Harry was looking for his skateboard. Doug just sat on his bike with one arm hanging over his handle bars, watching Terry.

Harry piped up, "Found it."

That snapped Terry out of his funk and he perked up his head, "Good, let's get this show on the road."

Doug was fine with Terry wanting to run the show and be their leader, he just wanted him to do so in a respectful and enjoyable manner. Also, not to hurt their other brother.

Harry was excited about this adventure. He had asked his brothers a few days ago if they could go to the top of South Table Mountain. Harry had heard from some of the other kids in class that you could see the whole Denver metropolitan area from the top, at the furthest east rock cliff. Plus, there was a chance to see deer, owls and many types of snakes that lived on the mountain. One of the kids said his dad saw a mountain lion up there one time, which Harry was hoping not to see.

The mountain itself was only about a quarter-mile away from where the Hamlins lived, but the neighborhood public access point was about a half-mile further. With it being that far away they decided to ride their bikes to the park entrance and leave them. There was a bike rack at the entrance that they could lock their bikes to. Harry would just have to throw his skateboard under a sage brush and hope nobody would steal it.

The cliff-top rock outcrop was visible from the entrance gate. It was extremely steep, only a little over 500 feet in elevation above them, but nearly straight up. The trail that zigzagged around to the backside of the rock outcropping and delivered you to the scenic spot was one-and-a-half miles long. The trail was mostly dirt, with some gravel areas where the dirt had washed away due to a rain storm.

Doug was carrying a backpack that had three canteens of water, a pair of binoculars and a camera. They figured it would take them at most an hour to get to the top. Then they could hang around, take pictures and maybe look for another rattle snake. This was Terry's reason for tagging along.

The day was a little warm. They would stop in the shade of the cottonwood trees once in a while and take a drink of water. Doug was making sure each of them was rationing their own canteen. He did not want them to run out

of water. Right when they got to the top,
Doug had to go. He looked around and
saw there was a section of tall shrubbery
about a hundred yards away.

"Hey guys, I have to go pee," he said as
he pointed and started walking to the
shrubs he was going to hide behind.

Terry and Harry nodded to Doug and
then started to walk up onto the top of the
rock outcropping. It was a truly amazing
view. A brilliantly blue sky continued all
the way to the horizon. The whole city was
visible from this one rock. Looking east,
you could see the skyscrapers in the
downtown area; Coors brewery and North
Table Mountain to the north. The taller
foothills, including Lookout Mountain with
all of the radio towers on it, was to the west.
And to the south you could see Chatfield
Reservoir and the top of Pikes Peak, which
was still white capped with snow.

Terry walked out real close to the edge
to look over and down toward their bikes.

Harry said, "Don't get so close to the
edge. You're making me nervous."

"Come on over here and take a look,"
said Terry.

Harry slowly shuffled his way to where
Terry stood and looked over the edge. He
immediately got a little woozy and fell to
his knees. He then reached down with his

hand to push himself back up off of a rock. The second his knees came up, the rock slid forward toward the cliff and so did Harry. He freaked, let out a squeak and turned back towards safety just in time to catch himself, but the rock was slippery from sand. His feet were skating and he quickly slid out to the edge of the rock outcropping. Harry just managed to stop himself from falling, thanks to a piece of granite rock that jutted out just enough to grab hold of.

He screamed and noticed that Terry was watching him the whole time from the safety of the trail, a strange smirk and look on his face. Terry dropped down on his butt and skidded to within a foot of Harry. Harry was elated to see his half-brother coming to his rescue. He reached his hand out to Terry, who just slapped it away. Harry thought Terry just missed his hand and again pushed it out but Terry who just sat there looking at it, his own hands below him on the rock he was sitting on. Terry did not make an effort to grab Harry's hand, or help him in anyway. He actually made a production of sniffing up some phlegm from his chest and spit it at Harry's extended hand, which was shaking.

Harry's fingers started slowly sliding on the moist moss that was wedged in between the cracks of the granite rock. Centimeter by centimeter, he felt his grip slipping.

"Terry, please help me," he squeaked.

He watched Terry look around, as if he was in trouble, then return his gaze to his eyes and smile. Terry didn't move a muscle. He was content on watching Harry slide off the rock into the abyss below. As if to further confirm that thought, Terry reached over and grabbed a loose pine cone off the forest floor.

Terry pulled his arm up slightly and looked at Harry. "Catch," he said and threw the pine cone.

Harry was in shock at this point and he did not even flinch as the pine cone hurled toward him. It nailed him right in the face, above his left eye. There was no pain. His shock was beyond that point. He kept staring at Terry, who sat there with that same smirk on his face and a slightly quizzical look. It was as if he was using Harry as an experiment. Terry grabbed and threw another pine cone, which hit him in what felt like the same place, just above his left eye. Now his eye stung a little bit and everything started getting blurry. There seemed to be a bright, reddish tint to everything he looked at. If he closed that eye, it helped the stinging and all the normal colors returned.

Harry tried to adjust his grip and scramble closer to safety but he made no progress. He began to succumb to his fate but still couldn't believe it was going to end like this. A member of his own family throwing pine cones at his face and watching him slide off a granite cliff to his death. He tried to look down below but he couldn't see the bottom; it was just a long straight wall that went into some shadows then into the black.

A huge hand came into view and threw Terry to the left and another hand; it looked to be a twin of the first, engulfed Harry's wrist and picked him up off the ledge like a Barbie doll. Harry saw Doug's wide eyes looking at him and that his mouth was moving, but he couldn't hear a sound.

For a moment, he thought he had fallen and was on his way down to his death. His last image was to be of his brother Doug. *Better than Terry,* he thought, *Terry didn't care if I dropped to my death.*

Chapter Twenty-Two

Jesse wanted to talk with John about his experience at the Walkers' home. He called his friend after his route to see if he was available later.

"Hey, John. What've you got going on this afternoon?"

"I have a feeling you are about to tell me."

"How about some hoops? I also need to run something by you."

"I'll be home by four."

"Thanks, John. See ya then."

John caught Jesse before he hung up, "Jesse, my dad got on me the other night, telling me I need to do more of the replenishing of our beer supply. He said I have the extracting part down. Can you pick up a case?"

"We don't have to drink beer," Jesse realized how lame it sounded right after it came out of his mouth.

"What? Do you want to meet at the library?" John giggled then said, "Hell, do you even know where one is?"

Jesse thought, *Really, what's with the library jokes lately?* Then he said, "All right, case of Coors Banquet on its way."

Jesse had gotten permission from Jane, the real estate agent, to visit the house and take some measurements inside. She had to meet him there with the lockbox combination and to supervise, since he was not yet the owner. Jane was helpful; she would hold one end of the tape measure for him and she offered some suggestions. He and Raven were curious how the few items they were taking from their existing homes would fit in their new one. Also, they were looking at purchasing some furniture. Jesse had printed out a diagram of the floor plan so he could measure some of the walls between doors and openings and write them down on the diagram.

This task had taken longer than he expected. It was just about 4:00 PM. Jesse said thanks and goodbye to Jane. He pulled up and parked on the street in front of John's house. The driveway was the basketball court so he had to leave that open. With it being such a warm day, he hoped the beer didn't get too warm sitting in his trunk. Jesse grabbed the case and walked it up to John who was already in the garage, lying on his back under the 1978 Ford Bronco he had rebuilt. Jesse wasn't sure John could ever be found in another part of the house.

"Hey Jesse, throw that beer in the fridge and grab a couple cold ones. I'll be done in a sec."

Jesse made himself at home sitting on John's tailgate with a beer in hand. John popped up from below, "Those damn brake calipers keep leaking."

Jesse cracked John a beer and handed it to him.

John smiled, "Good to see you, my friend. It's been a few."

"Sorry about that. Raven and I put in a bid on a home and they accepted."

"Congrats, Jesse. That's good news. We can have these talks in front of your beer fridge soon."

"I'll need to get a hoop, too. Where's the ball?"

"It popped."

"How did you manage that?"

"This kid kept driving by with his music too loud. I mean, you can hear him coming from a half mile away, ridiculous. Anyways, I had a few drinks in me and it popped against his right front fender while

I was politely asking him to turn down his music." John's sarcastic smile had emerged, "I've seen him speed by a couple of times lately and you couldn't even hear his radio."

"Well, I guess it worked, then. Did you ask him to buy you a new basketball?"

John giggled, "I've thought about it, but he is always in such a hurry to get past my place here I can't catch him."

"How's Melissa?"

"She's great as always, bringing some type of casserole over for dinner tonight. Funny you guys just bought a house together, I was thinking of asking Melissa to move in with me or us."

"Really? Is your dad fine with it?"

"Oh yeah, they spark up conversations and talk forever. I have to come out here for some peace. Plus, she's a hell of a chef. My dad thinks it would be great to have a woman in the house. It's been six years since Ma passed."

"Yeah, I remember. One year before my dad. Cool, well I hope Melissa is willing," Jesse giggled.

"Willing? More like reluctantly volunteering for service."

John took Jesse's beer can and as he was walking over to the recycling garbage pail he squished both cans flat at the same time in his large hands. This was always impressive. The cans were as flat as if you had set them on the ground and hard-stepped on their tops. He pulled two new cans from the fridge and tossed one to Jesse.

Jesse said, "So you know that girl I saved from being kidnapped...?"

John nodded, "Sure wish I was there."

"Well, it turns out that she penned a note for me and put it in their milk box," Jesse reached into his back pocket, pulled out a piece of yellow construction paper and handed it to John. John unfolded it and smiled at the simplicity of it, as well as the spelling.

"Really, is that how you spell your name?"

"Very funny."

John then developed a questioning look. "Hmmm, have you talked to her about this?"

"Very little, just when I was getting to the important questions her dad came home. He thought I was another kidnapper or something and started to come at me before his wife stopped him."

John nodded, "I guess you can't blame him there."

"Nope, just glad Karen showed up. Mr. Walker had a rusty spade fork in hand."

"Ryder is his name. I know him; well the shop I work for buys most of their auto parts from Ryder's store. He is actually a pretty nice guy and knows a lot about cars, too. Sometimes he will perform these magic tricks with your money when you are getting ready to pay. He is good at those, I haven't figured out how he does a single one of them."

"I saw the kid in the living room playing video games. He had a black eye and some scratches on his arms," Jesse paused, thinking on it. "Never said a word while I was there."

"Well, that doesn't necessarily mean the black eye was put there by Ryder. Maybe he plays a sport."

"Yeah, I know, but why would Haylee write that note? I did get to ask her how the black eye came about and she said, 'Sometimes Daddy gets mad, but he doesn't mean it'."

"My guess is it means nothing. Haylee saw Gary get spanked and yelled at twice in one week."

"She also said her mom is aware of the situation, but she just cries and drinks her special juice. For some reason I don't think its juice."

"Kids exaggerate, especially six-year-old kids. I understand that you can't let this go, I'd be mad at you too. But if you are going to mess with another family's dynamics, you better be careful. Ryder is not the type to sit back and cower."

"Yeah, where to start? Not sure talking with Haylee will accomplish much. I need to speak with Gary."

John again took Jesse's can, squished both then dropped them in the recycling bin and pulled two more out.

"That'll be hard without raising suspicion. I think you should meet the head of the snake first."

"What do you mean?"

"Don't you need some parts for your Firebird?"

"Ahhh, great idea."

Chapter Twenty-Three

"I'm not taking that shit bird kid that doesn't even respect me! Just Haylee," said Ryder.

Karen asked, "Well, how am I supposed to relax with him being around?"

"Let him go to that nerdy kid's place. What's his name?"

"Are you talking about Jeremy?"

"Who else? Isn't that his only friend?"

"Quit being so mean. It's not like you are inundated with friends."

"Whatever. He can hang out at Jeremy's place until I get back."

Ever since Gary sneezed while Ryder was approaching his highest bowling score, he had not taken Gary with him to the bowling alley on Wednesday evenings. He would make up some excuse or another but today he decided to tell his wife the truth.

Ryder was in good spirits, besides the drama with his step-son Gary. He considered the kid a mopey little cry baby but tolerated him due to his love for Karen. Sometimes, he actually wondered if it would have been better to let Gary live with his biological father. But Haylee also adored Gary and he didn't want to sadden her by severing that bond.

Ryder yelled down the hall to the bedrooms, "Haylee, are you about ready?"

He noticed Gary's door was shut and he figured Gary had heard him talking to his mom. He didn't care. The kid needed some tough love to make him stronger and get him ready for the real world.

"Just about, Daddy!"

A few seconds later, Haylee came running into the kitchen where Ryder and Karen waited. She said, "I almost forgot my purse."

Ryder smiled. He got a kick out of this. His little girl was growing up and trying to be lady-like in her mannerisms. Nowadays, she always wanted to make sure her hair was brushed and clothes were clean before she went out in public.

"OK, let's get to the car. We don't want to miss warm-ups."

Karen was busy flipping some grilled cheese sandwiches over a hot stove so he gave her a kiss on the cheek and followed Haylee out the screen door to the car, "See you in a few hours."

"Don't hurry back on my account," Karen replied.

A moment later, Gary came into the kitchen. Karen was plating two of the sandwiches, along with a bowl of tomato soup. This was a household favorite, mostly due to the simplicity of the meal. Gary sat down in his normal chair as his mom placed his food in front of him.

"Thanks, Ma. I heard Ryder." Gary did not call him Dad unless he was present, "And I already called Jeremy. He is expecting me in thirty minutes or so. I told him I was going to eat first."

"Sorry you had to hear that, Gary. He really does have a big heart and he does love you."

"Don't stick up for him, Mom. I want to be able to hold my dinner down."

Meanwhile, Ryder and Haylee were walking into the bowling alley. She saw where Ryder's teammates had congregated and ran over to them. They were always warm and engaged Haylee with questions. She would talk it up for quite some time after they arrived. Their neighbor, Jack, was her favorite. She would usually sit in his lap while telling everyone about her week.

Ryder sat down at the end of the bench and started getting ready, pulling out his shoes and ball. He would listen a little to what Haylee was saying but generally he tuned her out and started to focus on his game. The game of bowling was taken very seriously by Ryder, just as it had been by his father. It was the only sport that he had actually won a few trophies playing. All other sports that he tried, he felt clumsy, out of place, and he could never succeed.

Before the league games started, there was a period of warm-up for the players if they wanted. Ryder stood up on the wooden alley, ball in hand, focusing on the pins. His teammates knew how serious Ryder took the game and would hush up while he was in his approach stance. This was fine with them; he was a nice enough guy and always kept their team in the running for a win.

League play was underway. The chosen teams were paired off against one another, using the same ball return and scoring table for three games. It was the Auto Bachelors against the Beer Hounds. Ryder threw his first ball and he got what is called a Middle Finger. This is when the full rack of pins is hit but the five pin in the middle is the only one still standing. He proceeded to knock it down and complete the spare. He was not very happy about his first frame but his teammates encouraged him to shake it off.

The first game yielded Ryder with a one pin score above his average of 177. He was happy with the outcome, considering the start. Ryder headed back up to the lane, grabbing his ball; he was ready for the second game. This time he started out with a 'turkey' – three strikes in a row – and Ryder was elated, as were his teammates. In the fourth frame he picked up an easy spare, and then he proceeded to throw another turkey. Once again, Ryder was in range of breaking his all-time high.

Complimentary beers from his teammates were being stacked up near Ryder's chair, but he was slowly sipping on just one. He wanted to maintain his focus and coordination. Ryder ended the second game with a 248. He'd done it!

He jumped in the air and threw his fist high, "Yes!"

"Great game, Ryder!" yelled Cody.

"That is my new high score!"

"Oh wow, congrats! I didn't know," replied Cody.

Jack responded, "I don't think any of us realized that. Congrats, Ryder!"

Ryder stepped off the lane into the pit, heading for his chair, picking up the beer he had been nursing and throwing it down the hatch.

He grabbed another and swigged that one down in one gulp. A little beer rolled off his chin and onto the front of his shirt.

Ryder turned to Haylee, "Come give your dad a congratulatory hug."

Haylee grabbed a napkin as she ran to her father and jumped into his hands. She wiped away the beer on his shirt and a little off his chin, "You spilled some, Daddy."

The crew laughed, Ryder kissed Haylee on the forehead and set her back down. He started his third beer slower and continued his drinking through the last game, where he only managed to scrape by with a score of 135. He did not care. It was all about the high score.

"I think I'll cash in that rain check, guys," Ryder said to Jack and Cody, along with his other teammates.

Jack answered, "Of course! First round's on me."

By the time Ryder had polished his sixth beer at the bowling alley bar, Haylee was in the corner next to the juke box, sleeping. She was using her coat as a pillow and her father's as a blanket. Ryder was still celebrating and by this time he was slurring his words, stumbling around and spilling beer on the floor as well as other patrons.

"Hey, Ryder, why don't you take your little girl home and then come back?" asked Cody.

Jack had been paying attention and curbed his drinking, in anticipation of giving Ryder and Haylee a ride home. He watched Ryder return from the restroom. As he approached his bar stool, he fell down to his knees and spilled the rest of his beer on the floor.

The bar keep spoke up, "Hey Ryder, you are cut off."

"Screw you, Joe!"

Jack walked over and helped Ryder to stand and held him steady, "C'mon Ryder, let's go home."

"No way, Jack. I want another beer."

"Haylee is waking up now. Do you want her to see you in this state?" asked Jack.

Ryder reared his arm back and even though he was drunk, he could still throw a punch. It caught Jack on the left side of his chin and knocked him back into Cody and the others who were sitting on the bar stools.

Joe reached for the phone, "Calling the police, Ryder!"

Ryder said, "C'mon, Haylee. Time to split."

Haylee ran up, grabbing her dad's hand, and they jogged out the front door of the bowling alley. Some of the drunkenness must have worn off at the mention of police; he seemed to be moving fine now. They jumped in the car and took off.

Joe hung up the phone; he hadn't even dialed. "Boy, that guy needs to learn to stop at four. How're you doing, Jack?"

Jack was rubbing his chin, "I'm all right. He sure can throw a powerful punch though. Set me up with one more, Joe."

Joe pointed to the corner where Haylee had been sleeping, "Will do. Looks like he left his bowling bag again."

Ryder went undetected by the police on this trip home and luckily did not crash with Haylee in the car. He walked up the steps behind his daughter and unlocked the front door.

"Go get ready for bed, darling."

"OK, Daddy. Good night."

"Good night, sweetheart."

Ryder was too excited to go to bed. He was still pumped up from breaking his high score and getting into a fight. Being drunk didn't help matters. He walked out to the living room to talk with Karen and share his story. To his disappointment, she was passed out drunk on the couch with the television blaring; something about a new type of food processor. Ryder found the remote and flipped the channel to watch the rerun of the Colorado Rockies game played earlier in the day. He looked at Karen, who had her mouth open and was snoring.

After grabbing a bag of unshelled roasted peanuts from the cupboard, Ryder returned to the living room and sat in the lazy boy chair across from Karen. He reclined the chair and kicked his feet up before realizing that he forgot a bowl to hold the peanut shells. Not wanting to get back up, he was tempted to yell for Gary and make the sniveling cry baby wake up to get him a bowl. But he decided against that, because Gary would just ruin his high.

Ryder always had enjoyed the game of darts, even though he was not very good. However, he decided that this opportunity posed as a perfect time for some much needed practice. After cracking open a peanut shell to retrieve the treasure within, he would place the empty shell between his thumb and index finger. Then he would loft it through the air, trying to get the shell into Karen's mouth. Sometimes, it would land on her face and she would brush it away as though it were a fly. By the time Ryder finished the one-pound bag, the front of Karen's shirt was covered with peanut shells. They were tangled in her hair, lying on the couch around her, and some made it to the carpeted floor. Ryder decided to go to bed since the Rockies were losing badly and he finally felt tired. He lifted Karen's arm just enough to slide the roasted peanuts bag under, to make it look like she was the one eating the nuts.

Haylee awoke the next morning to find her mom still asleep on the couch, holding an empty peanut bag. There were peanut shells all over the place. She ran into Gary's room.

"Gary, come see this!"

He was awake reading in his bed. "OK, one sec."

They walked back out to the living room together and started laughing. Karen's eyes were starting to flutter open.

Gary said loudly, "Mom, you ate all the peanuts! C'mon, you know we like them, too."

"Yeah, Mommy!" Haylee piped in.

Chapter Twenty-Four

Through an open window at 2:30 in the morning, sounds were more pronounced and recognizable. Jesse had left his Firebird outside on the driveway because he was using the garage to work on refinishing a desk that his father had built. There was a noticeable slow quiet squeak that sounded like the noise he heard when he opened his driver-side door. Currently, he was not able to lock his car, since the ignition key did not match the door key. Not thinking straight, he had thrown the door key away when he replaced the ignition, while the car was still on blocks in the garage. Nobody had previously messed with his car.

Hurriedly, he pulled on his pants and tied his shoes and, without turning on any lights, made his way to the front window that overlooked the driveway. The dome light was on in his Firebird and he could see somebody inside it, looking around. There was the silhouette of another person standing by the mail box at the end of the driveway with his back to the house. He thought, *Must be the sentinel.*

Jesse went to the front door, quietly unlocked it, and was slowly opening the door to try to remain undetected. All of a sudden a bright light flashed, illuminating the two perpetrators for a couple of seconds, then was just as quickly extinguished.

"Troy," Jesse muttered as he sprinted out the door. The two trespassers took to running north. Jesse slammed his car door shut as he ran by, to save the battery.

Jesse was gaining on them quickly. The smaller of the two was faster, with a good thirty-yard lead on his accomplice. At the end of the block, each of them turned a different direction as planned, so only one of them would get caught if a chase ensued. He decided on the bigger one. Just as Jesse was closing in and ready to tackle his prey, the trespasser turned slightly and stuck his leg out to try and trip Jesse. A last-second jump over the outstretched leg saved Jesse from flying flat-out onto the concrete sidewalk. At this point the trespasser was extremely winded, stopped running and stood in the middle of the sidewalk, lowering his shoulders and raising his fists.

Jesse turned around to face his opponent, walking directly towards him with his hands at his side. "Look, I'm already running late. Why don't you just apologize?"

The guy had a large nose, which spread across a good portion of his face. He was nearly Jesse's size, with dark hair that was offset by intense blue eyes. There was a scar that stretched from the top of his right ear down to his chin.

"Arrrrrgggghhhhhh…" his opponent started screaming and running directly at Jesse in a bull rush.

Jesse waited until the man was nearly on him, then he nonchalantly stepped to the left, grabbed the back of the guy's bent over-head, and slammed his knee directly into his face. Something had popped with that hit. He let go of the guy immediately after the blow, to watch him drop onto his back in a grassy area next to the curb.

The trespasser was rolling back and forth, side to side on the ground, holding his bloody nose, "My nose! Arghhhh. Damn you!"

Jesse didn't care to stand around and watch or listen to this guy. He looked to see where the other perpetrator went but he was out of sight.

"Hmmm, three blocks. This guy was pretty quick," Jesse said to himself as he walked back to his house.

Troy saw Jesse returning and came barging out of his front door to ask, "Hey Jesse, did you catch them?"

"Of course, Troy."

"I got their pictures in full HD. They both stupidly looked directly at the light before the camera flashed."

"That's great. Can you send that picture to my email?"

Troy was anxiously happy for Jesse's approval and attention, "Sure, Jesse, will do. I saw them walking on the other side of the street looking in cars an hour ago at 1:15 AM."

"Man, Troy, don't you ever sleep?"

Troy pulled up, looking a little embarrassed about this question. He had helped Jesse in the past with his constant surveillance of the neighborhood, but he was very sensitive to the idea of being considered a neighborhood spy and didn't want anyone to think of him as a nosy neighbor.

Jesse caught his stunned look. "No worries, Troy. It was an honest question, not an accusation."

"Oh, OK. I do sleep hard through the morning hours, but I love to watch what stirs at night."

"Thanks again, Troy, I need to make some coffee and get to work. Can you let me know if you see either of those guys around here again?"

Troy smiled, it made him feel useful, given a task even this small, "I sure will, Jesse."

Jesse decided to drive the Firebird since he was running late. When he drove, he usually took the same long route that he enjoyed on his bike. There were a couple of paved stretches where there were rarely any other cars at such an early hour. He would stop right in the middle of the road, drop it into first gear keeping the clutch pushed in, rev up the motor to 3000 RPMs then drop the clutch and gun it. The rear of the car would rise up, start fish-tailing, and white rubber smoke would be fogging up the area. Then he would shoot out of the fog like a rocket and shut it down after he hit 80 mph. Jesse loved muscle cars and was hoping to enter his Firebird into a race at Bandimere Speedway sometime.

His delivery route was uneventful; just the way he liked it. Pull to a stop at the house, verify with the customer order list, gather the items from the back, transport them to the milk box, empty the milk box of any recyclables or returns, place the new order into the milk box, and transport the old ones back to the recycle bin in the truck. Then on to the next house. It was mundane but he enjoyed the physical attribute of his job and Mr. Roman paid well.

When he would drive his car to work, Fran would place the care basket on the front passenger seat. She would also purposely roll up his windows so the pleasant fragrance would permeate the interior. He had told Fran that this was cruel and unusual punishment but she feigned innocence. She had claimed that Gabrielle was delivering the basket to his car. When he asked Gabrielle, she would say it was Fran. This morning it was easy to decipher what the care basket contained.

At home, Jesse was ascending the front porch and heard the television playing the theme music for *The Price is Right*, which made him smile.

He burst through the door. "Good morning, Ma. We got biscuits and gravy!"

Becky looked up from the television, "Good morning, Jesse. That sounds wonderful."

Jesse was in the kitchen, reheating the gravy in a pot and the biscuits in the toaster oven. He yelled out to the front room, "You want an egg on top, Ma?"

"Please, over easy and right on top of the gravy over the biscuit." Becky liked the egg incorporated into the food, not sitting on the side.

Jesse plated up the biscuits and gravy, throwing an egg on top of each plate. Then he dropped a few ice cubes into two glasses and poured them each a glass of orange juice. It dawned on him that he had not tried out his latest prank. He opened the highest cabinet that his mom could not reach, pulling out a fake ice cube that had a fake fly in the middle of it. When placed in the glass of orange juice it looked surprisingly real.

Jesse carried out the two plates then went back to retrieve the drinks. Becky grabbed the glass of orange juice and just before she took a drink she looked into the glass then made a squishy face in disgust.

"What? Now you don't like my cooking?"

She reached across the table, grabbing Jesse's orange juice glass and pushed hers over to him. Becky smiled with satisfaction, "There, you need the extra protein more than I do."

Jesse laughed, fetching the fake ice cube out with his spoon, "See, just a prank, Ma."

"Biscuits and gravy is nothing to prank about, young man. Now, quit with the revelry and let me watch my show. Since you seem to be into alternative forms of protein now, I'll go grab an earth worm from the garden for your dinner plate," Becky replied in her sarcastic manner.

He threw his hands up in front of him, "All right, I give."

They ate in silence, except for Drew Carey hosting *The Price is Right* and Becky lightly humming while she consumed one of her favorite breakfasts.

Jesse had planned to drive over to the auto part store that Ryder worked at and meet the guy in a different environment. John had told him that Ryder seemed like a decent man and that he should meet the head of the snake before passing judgement. Besides, the Firebird has had some sporadic misfiring problems which he believed to be the spark plug wires. The store was not any further than the one he usually frequented.

Ryder was standing outside the auto part store, looking under the hood of an old beat-up Chevy pickup with another man when Jesse pulled into the parking lot. He turned off his Firebird, sitting and watching as the two poked around the engine compartment. Ryder seemed to take control and had found something; he stood fully erect and talked with the pickup owner while cleaning his hands with a rag. The two of them left the hood up and walked back into the store. There were other people milling around, with one other clerk to aid. Ryder went behind the counter, lost among the shelves of parts for a few minutes, and returned with a small box. He stepped behind the cash register and the pickup owner paid for the part. Ryder came back out with the owner carrying the box and a wrench. He positioned himself against the front grille and reached down, using the wrench, pulling out an old greasy, grimy part. Wiping his hands on a rag, he removed the new part from the box then reached down and secured it. Ryder then instructed the owner to start the truck, which fired up right away. Jesse watched Ryder nod to himself in satisfaction, slam the hood shut, then walk over to the smiling owner's window and shake his hand.

Jesse stepped into the store and got in line at the parts counter, behind two other gentlemen. He purposely picked the spark plug wires because they were always behind the counter instead of being out on the floor. This way, he would have to talk with someone behind the counter. Currently, it was either Ryder or, according to his name tag, a man named Henry. As the line shrunk, Jesse noticed that he was going to get Henry as a helper. He stepped to the side and motioned for the guy behind him to step in front of him.

"Ah, the milk man," Ryder stuck his hand out for a shake. "Was it Jerry?"

"Close, but Jesse. I get that one a lot."

"Look I want to apologize about my aggressive nature the other day. I truly thought you were another kidnapper and were there to harm my daughter." Ryder seemed sincere.

"Yeah, I can imagine how it looked with the recent dealing of a true kidnapper. No worries, just glad Karen was there."

Ryder pointed, "Is that your Firebird?"

"Yep." Jesse thought, *Hmmm, there are close to a dozen cars out there. How would he know unless he had noticed me already?*

"Very nice, what's under the hood?"

Jesse liked to brag about his car, "A 400, but I modified it a bit. It's pushing out 370 horsepower. Runs the quarter-mile in under twelve seconds."

Ryder whistled lightly. "Whew, nice. Always been a fan. So, what can I help you with today?"

"I'd like to try some of those 8mm Taylor plug wires you have behind the counter."

"Are you arcing?"

"A couple wires are but not consistently."

"How old are the wires and what's the brand?"

"Bosch wires, they're a couple years old, but miles wise, I'd say 5000."

"Are the wires held tight and separated by anything?"

"Not really, they're hanging loose for the most part."

"I consider Bosch a good brand and that is not old for spark plug wires. Those Taylor wires you want are over one hundred dollars and not guaranteed to solve the problem. I'd suggest trying some Moroso plug wire separators and some Thermo-Tec plug wire sleeves and you can get out of here under thirty bucks. My guess is there are some wires crossing paths and they are not separated enough or getting too hot. Even if it does not fully fix your problem, this is something you'll want to do for a machine like that."

"Hmmm, OK, that sounds good. Let me try that first."

"One minute," Ryder said as he turned and went back to the part shelves, returning less than a minute later. "OK, here we go. Now, do you know how to install these or would you like some help? We can do it right in the parking lot, take about five minutes."

Jesse thought, *Well, I'm sure I can figure out how to install these, but this will give me a chance to get to know him better.*

"Actually, I would appreciate a little help."

"That'll be $28.38," Ryder supplied the change. "Let me grab a couple of tools and let's go install these."

Jesse popped the hood when they got there as Ryder viewed the full compartment, "Very nice, sure is fun to see an old muscle car in such pristine shape without any rust."

Ryder bent over prodding and handling the spark plug wires to test their movement. "Yeah, see there, these wires need to be held in place or when they touch they can arc. Also, those two wires are too close to the intake manifold, which could make them too hot." He started pulling the wires apart and putting the separators in place.

Jesse couldn't think of how to ask Ryder if he beat his kids, "So is it just, Haylee?"

Ryder answered while he was working, "Nope, raising a teenage boy, too."

"Two and one is a teenager. That must be tough?"

Ryder stood erect and looked at Jesse, "Yeah, nothing to take lightly. You got anymore car questions?"

"No, but I have to ask, what was Haylee doing clear over on Federal Boulevard, alone?"

"That's none of your business, Jesse," Ryder grabbed the top of the hood, pulled it down, then in a mean-spirited tone, "Keep

your nose out, boy, and remember your place,
Milk-man."

Chapter Twenty-Five

Lately, Doug had been experiencing anxiety attacks. They generally happened after he had been on a multiple-day drunken stupor. There was this overwhelming feeling of an impending doom approaching, but if he cut out the sauce the feeling would disappear by the next morning. He had been to the doctor's office after ten years of neglect. The doctor took some blood tests, the results to be revealed later, and then sent him home with a prescription to help with his anxiety. Instead of filling the prescription, Doug decided to try the sober route for a week.

After the first week he noticed his sleeping habits improved. He felt much better and had not once awoken in the alley behind his garage, his coat as a makeshift pillow. This situation was not uncommon when Doug was drinking. Sometimes, he would awaken to his front door wide open, and once a raccoon was sitting on his couch, eating the last of a bag of Fritos. About a year ago, he had woken up to the most awful screeching coming from the front room. He grabbed a bat, snuck down the hall and peaked around the corner. There were no less than six magpies fighting over a bag of popcorn he had left on the couch. It was quite the feat to reclaim his territory; needless to say, the clean-up of the shredded popcorn and excrement took some time.

Once a month of soberness rolled around, Doug was really enjoying his new-found freedom, unstrapped from the bar stool. The fog in his mind started to clear. He was again enjoying the little things in life. He could hear the birds chirping, the children playing in the park, and his taste buds had come back to life. His favorite meal was a big bowl of spaghetti, which he had not been able to taste or even remember eating in the last seven years.

There was just one regret that kept popping into his mind; Gary. What had happened with Karen made his heart ache, but he felt that leaving the boy as he did was not acceptable. Besides, over the last year Karen had started drinking rather heavily herself. She would join Doug at the bar a couple of days a week, when he would hand her some of the alimony money he owed.

Doug kept rolling different ideas through his head as to how he could reconnect with Gary. There was no way he could enter the bar again to meet Karen and trust that he could exit the establishment sober. He really wanted to talk to her first, though, because he was unsure how he would be received by Gary. *Geez I must owe her two months of alimony.*

When he decided to try to get sober, one of the first things he did was turn in his phone and get a new one with a new number and none of the tempting old contacts. His bar patron friends kept calling him and he needed that to end. If he wanted to talk to them again, he knew where they were. The layout of the bar was easy for him to picture, as well as each stool the regulars would occupy. Karen might be mad at him; the phone was how she would keep in touch so she would not have been able to make contact at all.

He could not remember her number so he decided to walk down to Karen's home and stand outside on the sidewalk for a minute to see if he was noticed. This wasn't something new; he had been walking by their house for close to a month. Always when he knew Ryder was at work. He kept hoping to catch a glimpse of his son, but he wasn't even sure Gary would recognize him. One time as he approached their home, Karen came out the front door. Doug had turned quickly and acted like he was looking at something in a tree. Nervous and unsure of what to say, he had continued back toward his home.

This time, it only took two minutes before Karen saw him, from her living room couch. He waved at her from the sidewalk. She came out looking around suspiciously but her smile was intact, which relieved Doug immensely.

Karen asked, "Are you ok?

"Yes, actually I can't remember feeling better."

She tilted her head as she approached, her smile growing, "I tried to call you a few times."

"Sorry about that. It took me a while to get to where I am at, and losing the phone was a big part of it."

Now Karen frowned quizzically, "Well you look good. Your eyes are clear."

"I've been sober for over a month, Karen."

"Oh my goodness. Congratulations, Doug!"

"Thank you."

"What brings you here?"

Doug handed Karen a check, "Last month's alimony. And…"

"And… what?"

"I would like to reconnect with Gary."

"Oh geez, I'm not sure how Ryder would react to you coming over. Why after all these years, now?"

"I'm no longer a drunk and realize what an idiot I have been. And it doesn't have to be here. He could come over to my place or we could meet in a park."

"I'm not sure he wants to ever see you again."

Doug looked down at the sidewalk, "I know. I have put a lot of thought into that, but I still have to at least try."

"Well, it's not my position to say no. I will ask Gary and let you know, but I am not involving Ryder. How can I get in touch with you?"

Doug handed her a piece of paper that had his new phone number on it. "Ryder will have to be involved. He needs to remove the restraining order he put on me."

"What?"

"Don't worry about it. Maybe he was right. I was mad and drunk back then. Eventually, the mad turned into sad, but the drunk never went away."

"I don't know if I can tell Ryder. He is scary sometimes."

"I'll take care of Ryder, but I would appreciate if you could see how Gary responds to the idea. If he is not onboard, then there is no reason to proceed. I have never lost my love for him, Karen."

"You have a funny way of showing it."

"There is a restraining order, Karen. I cannot be within fifty feet of Gary."

"Not even a birthday or Christmas present, Doug?"

Doug looked down again, "That is my bad, Karen. Please do this for me?"

"OK, Doug. You have to remain sober, though."

"Ha. When's the last drink you had?"

"This isn't about me."

"Sorry, that was out of line."

Karen smiled at him.

Doug turned, started to walk away, then said over his shoulder, "Not to push you or anything, but I know a great little AA meeting on Tuesdays, if you are ever interested."

Haylee came in from the back yard, calling for her mom. She started walking room to room, hoping she wasn't passed out somewhere from the special juice. She peeked out the front window and saw her mom talking to a strange man on the sidewalk. He had turned and started walking away while Karen remained, watching after him.

Haylee caught her mom at the door, "Who was that?"

"That my dear was, Doug Hamlin, but don't tell your father he was here."

Haylee smiled and made the zipper motion across her mouth. "I won't." She ran back to the window to watch him walk the rest of the way down the block.

Chapter Twenty-Six

Doug and Harry were sitting on the couch in the front room again, their game controllers in hand. The television was busy making loud booms, bangs, and the occasional scream. Both of them were mesmerized by their game.

"You guys want to go drink at the tree house again? I just looked, there's a whole twelve-pack in the refrigerator."

Doug replied, "Jesus, Terry. Don't you ever learn? Maybe I should go stick you in the trunk right now."

Terry shook and dropped his head in a mopey fashion.

"Sorry man, that was mean," Doug said, "But Harry and I are tired of watching these episodes with Dad."

Terry perked back up, "Snake hunting?"

Harry said, "I don't want to be pooped on today."

"I know we only have two poles, but we could go fish the pond."

Doug stood up and dropped his controller onto the coffee table, "I'm in."

"All right, me too," Harry agreed as he turned off the television.

The Hamlin brothers loaded up with their two rods and a tackle box full of various fish attractants. Being the responsible one, Doug filled up three canteens to carry in his back pack. While he was in the kitchen, Doug opened up the refrigerator, pulled out six beers and stowed them alongside the water.

A huge elm tree supplied shade on one side of the pond. It was only six blocks away, which made it an easy walk; there was too much gear to carry on their bikes. The spot they always chose was in the shade, with a grassy bank and a nice comfortable log that was more than long enough for all three of them to use as a back support.

Bluegills were the usual affair, but once in a while a large mouth bass would take the bait. They didn't plan on keeping any fish so they left the stringer and creel at home. Harry grabbed one of the poles; he usually liked to walk around the pond a couple of times, throwing his lure into different spots. Doug caught two fish then handed the rod to Terry and leaned back against the log to relax. Terry preferred to sit so he dressed the pole up with a bobber and hung a worm about two feet under it. There was a set of rocks he had placed at the edge of the pond a few years ago that would hold a pole up and stay in place once a fish was on. Terry leaned back against the log next to Doug.

Doug asked, "Thirsty?"

"Yeah, I'm a bit dry."

Terry heard a zipper then the sound of a carbonated beverage in an aluminum can being cracked opened. He looked over at Doug to see him holding a beer out in his direction. Terry smiled, "All right! You dog."

Doug smiled as he popped his own beer then rose it up in a 'cheers motion', "Now this is fishing."

"Hell, yeah."

Harry was oblivious to his brothers drinking on the far bank. Doug wanted it that way. He planned on drinking three of them and was sure Terry would do the same. Harry was not a good drunk; besides, he was enjoying himself fishing. About the only time Doug could stand Terry was while they were drinking. They were mostly silent during the first beer, watching Harry reel in a couple of fish and hold them up so they could see it.

Doug would yell at him, "Nice fish. Catch another."

That kept Harry on the far side of the pond while Doug and Terry drank the beer. When the second beers were cracked open, they got a little chattier with one another. Talking about different girls in their school and which sports they hoped to sign up for this coming fall. They were laughing and carrying on with one another.

Harry looked over a couple of times and noticed they had beer cans. He didn't want to participate so he kept fishing on the far side of the pond.

"Doug, we got a bite!" Terry yelled as he jumped up and ran over to the pole that was stuck in the rocks by its handle. When he bent over to grab the handle he got dizzy and fell face-first into the pond, completely missing the fishing pole.

"I'll get it!" Doug was laughing at Terry as he lunged forward and because of the uncontrollable laughter he tripped over the rock pile and did a belly flop right next to Terry.

The two of them started laughing harder and splashing each other.

Harry walked over to reel in the fish and let it go, "You guys are ruining the fishing."

"We'll catch fish the old-fashioned way, with our teeth," Terry replied as he went back under the water.

Doug said, "Come on in, Harry. It's nice and cool in here."

"No thanks. You guys will dunk me and pull my pants off, I'm going home."

Harry gathered his things, along with his favorite of the two fishing poles, so his brothers wouldn't break it, and started the trek home. Doug and Terry made their way to the bank and pulled themselves out of the pond.

"Boy, that felt good," Terry said.

"Yes, it did. Come on, we got one more beer each."

"Sweet!"

Both of them pulled off their shirts and hung them on branches in the sun to dry. Doug pulled out the remaining two beers. He and Terry both assumed their previous positions, sitting on the bank, leaning back against the old Cottonwood log.

"So what makes you do it, Terry?"

"What do you mean?"

"Why do you constantly defy Dad? I mean, he gives one hell of a punishment."

"I don't consider him my father, Gary. Just a lug my mom ended up with." Terry was silent for a minute looking out across the pond, "I won't be sticking around much longer, anyways."

"What? Where are you going?"

"Look man, I don't have a death wish, Doug. And by the way your dad's beatings keep increasing in violence; I need to get the hell out of dodge."

"He's your father, too."

Terry giggled sarcastically, "Oh no he's not. He has told me so many times."

"What about your mom and us?"

"What about it? It's not going to do either one of us any good if I'm dead."

Doug turned to look back at the pond. He knew Terry was right and that made him sad. Even though he was mean to Harry, he felt a strong kinship with Terry. Also, he figured that mean side would soften with age, especially once they were out of their parents' home and living on their own.

Each of them finished off their last sip of beer. Doug grabbed the cans, throwing them into his backpack; he was not a fan of litter. Terry stood up once Doug had pulled his back pack on over his shoulders. After gathering the rest of the gear, they both started the trek home in silence.

About halfway home Terry said, "It won't be so bad, I'll write to you and Harry and of course my mom."

"Hope so."

"Of course I will, you guys will be a happier family, too. I bet your dad calms down and the house becomes violence-free."

The rest of the walk home was silent. As they got into view of the house they noticed Nick's car was gone. This pleased both of them. A nap to sleep off the high they were coming down from would set them right.

Doug was awakened when he heard some yelling and decided to get up and investigate. As he stepped into the kitchen he saw that Nick had his belt off, with Terry sitting on a chair in front of him, crying.

Nick yelled, "Just rest assured, Terry, every beer in this house will be accounted for from now on!"

Doug said, "I took the beers Dad not Terry."

"I don't care, I am sure he was the instigator," Nick retorted. "Now shut up and leave us be." He looked back at Terry, "In fact, get your ass up, we're taking this outside."

Harry was on the couch in the front room, watching some cartoon when Doug sat down next to him. Doug and Harry heard yelling outside on the driveway along with a couple of smacking noises then the all-too-familiar sound of a trunk slamming.

Chapter Twenty-Seven

This Sunday was reserved to move Raven and Jesse into their new home. One of the several cars that John had access to was a pickup truck. Both he and Mr. Roman backed into the Martins' driveway to load up Raven's belongings. Between Mr. Roman, Roger, John, Carl and Jesse the loading went quickly; besides, Raven did not have much in the way of possessions. Neither did Jesse. Apart from their bedrooms, most of the furniture was going to be purchased from a second-hand store at a later date.

After they had delivered Raven's belongings, Jesse and Mr. Roman headed over to his place to gather Jesse's belongings. Only one truck was needed for his worldly possessions. John stayed back to help move the items into the house to their pre-determined locations.

As housewarming gifts, Fran donated two full-length couches that had been under a tarp in their basement for a few years. She also had a couple of boxes for their kitchen, which included place settings, glasses, a few pots and pans and an old percolating coffee pot, which Jesse was all too happy to see. Becky bought them a nice kitchen table with four chairs. The Martins bought them a whole entertainment center with a stereo sound bar and a sixty-inch television. Jesse and Raven marveled at this gift.

Carl said, "Well, when I visit, I want to be able to keep up on the Rockies score."

With the kitchen appliances being left behind by the previous owners, Jesse and Raven felt they were in reasonably good shape for the moment. They were able to cook, store food, and sleep comfortably.

Towards the end of the move, as the last of the boxes were being hauled inside, people were starting to phase out and become tired. Without saying a word, Fran and Becky disappeared in Jerry's truck. Everyone else had finished bringing in the leftover items; most of it was stacked up in the garage to be dealt with at a later time.

They all crowded around the two couches; some were sitting on the ground. Fran and Becky returned shortly, to everyone's delight, with four large pepperoni pizzas, a roll of paper towels, and three cases of beer. The beer cases were the first to be attacked and the pizza was just as big a hit. They all began to relax, reveling in the new home, slices of pizza plated on paper towels, beers in hand. Gradually, people started to say their goodbyes and filter home. John of course was the last to leave; there was still beer to be drunk. But eventually, Jesse and Raven were alone.

The only source of entertainment that Jesse had hooked up was the stereo. He turned it on and joined Raven sitting on the couch.

She stretched out and laid her head on his leg, "I can't believe this is really ours."

"I know. It looks like a tornado went through here, but we'll get it fixed up soon enough."

"I'm not worried about that. We have all the time in the world. We are together now."

Jesse kissed her forehead.

Raven asked, "So have you been able to talk with young Haylee any further?"

"That sure is a hard one to read. The father seems nice enough, but he doesn't like to talk about his family. The boy does have the markings of a fight or some contact sport. I am not sure if Haylee is over-exaggerating a punishment that Ryder delivered to Gary or if it is real."

"He may just like his privacy."

"If he is innocent, I don't want to raise awareness to the authorities and cause the family more problems. Don't you think a neighbor or passerby would have heard or seen something?"

"People are afraid to get mixed up in other people's troubles nowadays."

"The one thing that still bothers me is when I asked Haylee about Gary's black eye. She seemed very sincere when she said, 'Sometimes Daddy gets mad. He doesn't mean it.' "

"Hmm, if she worded it in that manner, that doesn't sound good. Can you just ask Gary?"

Chapter Twenty-Eight

Jesse decided to ride his bike to work on this brisk summer morning. A slight cool down had taken hold of Colorado and temperatures were going to be twenty degrees cooler than average. This happened a few times each summer; it was a blessed relief from the sweltering heat.

As he pulled into the gravel lot at Romans' Dairy, he noticed a strange car parked just to the left of the lot entrance. Somebody was sitting in the car, looking towards the drivers that were loading their trucks. Jesse slowed his bike down to get a better view through the windshield. *Is that Ryder? It does look like his car.*

Ryder finally faced forward and saw Jesse looking at him as he slowly rode by. Jesse stopped the bike as Ryder rolled down the window.

"Good morning, Mr. Walker."

"I know where you work, Jesse." Ryder flipped him off and yelled out, "Right back at you pal."

Ryder started the car and took off in a cloud of dust.

Jesse thought, *Very odd, what the hell was that about? This guy is missing a few screws upstairs.*

"Who the hell was that?"

Jesse turned to see Mr. Roman advancing onto the scene. Mr. Roman had a Colt 45 pistol holstered on his right side; he carried that pistol around the dairy most days. Foxes and coyotes would get after the chickens. Rattle snakes were spotted out in the pasture and sometimes next to the house, where his granddaughters played.

"This guy I recently met."

Mr. Roman said, "He had been sitting out here for nearly thirty minutes. Then when you showed up and stopped next to him I decided to investigate." He looked at Jesse as the red tail lights were disappearing. "You look a bit miffed?"

"I was not expecting that at all."

"Is he a threat?"

"I guess … I'm not sure."

His deliveries went without adversity. He had planned to set up the rest of the entertainment system in the afternoon to hopefully allow Raven and him to watch television. He thought, *After all of these years, I'm not really sure there is another station besides the Gameshow Network…?*

As he dropped his bike in the front yard of his mom's home he saw Troy waving to him through his front room bay window. He held his finger up, gesturing for Jesse to wait one minute. Troy came out and walked over to the edge of his yard.

"Jesse, I hear you are moving away."

"Yes, I already have, Troy."

"Well, that's a bummer."

"I'll be coming around quite often still, Troy, just as I am here now. I would really appreciate if you could help keep watch on my mom to make sure she is safe."

Troy took this as a compliment, "Of course, Jesse. How do I contact you?"

"I only moved, Troy. I didn't sell everything and flee to a monastery. My cell phone is the same number."

"Oh, ok. Thanks, Jesse."

The care basket contained a more simplistic brunch this morning. Jesse pulled out the poaching pods, making some poached eggs with toast and a glass of apple juice. He hung around for another twenty minutes, talking to his mom, until he was done cleaning the dishes.

Kissing his mom on the cheek he said, "I'll see ya tomorrow morning, Ma."

Jesse pulled into his new driveway and thought, *Hmm, maybe I need to plant an evergreen bush by the front door to hide my bike.* He stepped inside, turned on the radio and headed for the shower. Soon, he would have to decide if he wanted to register and continue with his college courses. He kept leaning toward the idea of taking a semester off, with all that was going on in his life.

There were a few beers left over from the move-in day and Jesse thought that sounded good while hooking up the rest of the entertainment center. He opened the refrigerator to see that Raven had left her lunch box. Since he had just showered, he decided against making the delivery on his Schwinn, it would only cause him to sweat.

Jesse stepped through the emergency entrance carrying a pink lunch box with a unicorn on the side; quite the sight he imagined. He spotted Raven talking to a couple of colleagues at the far end of the hallway and he noticed two of them watching him approach.

One of them tapped her arm, "Raven, check out this hunk."

Raven saw the direction her friends were looking then smiled, "That's my hunk."

Connie muttered, "Very nice. You must introduce us."

Raven stepped over to meet Jesse. They hugged and kissed.

Raven asked, "What are you doing here?"

Jesse held up his arm, "You left this at home."

"Oh that's so sweet," Raven smiled. "Did you feel tough walking in here carrying that?"

"Never more so!"

"Come on over here, meet a couple of friends."

They stepped over to her two friends who were blushing lightly.

"Connie, this is Jesse." They shook hands. "Rhonda, this is Jesse."

Rhonda was a little bold, "If you ever decide to leave this woman, you know where to find me."

Connie slapped Rhonda's shoulder, "Rhonda!" Her friend just giggled.

Raven took that as a compliment. Everywhere she went with Jesse, she noticed the girls watching him. He seemed completely oblivious to it.

The automatic doors that Jesse had stepped through whisked open and a medic yelled down the hall, "I need help!"

Jesse was ahead of the nurses and the first out the door.

The medic said, "I can't lift this gurney by myself, the patient is too big."

Jesse grabbed one end to help the medic pull the gurney out and drop the wheels into place. Right then, the three nurses showed up to start wheeling the patient into the hospital. Raven smiled and waved bye as she was helping with the gurney. He turned to look at the medic, who had just shut the rear doors of the ambulance.

The medic held out his hand, "Thanks, mister. I'm Edward."

Accepting the hand shake, Jesse replied, "Sure, Edward. I'm Jesse."

Chapter Twenty-Nine

"Gary, would you please answer the door? My hands are full," Karen yelled from the laundry room.

"Sure, Ma." Gary set down his video game controller to answer the door bell.

"Hi, Mr. Peterson."

"Good morning, Gary. How are you doing?" After Jack finished his sentence, upon closer inspection he noticed the black eye and bruising on Gary's arms.

"I'm doing ok, trying to master a video game to show up Jeremy."

"I don't mean to pry, Gary, but did you get into a fight at school? Is that why you are home?"

"Uh no, Mr. Peterson, that was from a mishap here involving the stairs and one of Haylee's doll toys."

Karen heard the exchange and realized she had forgotten about Gary's injuries. *Oh shoot!*

Karen hurried to the door and showed up behind Gary looking a little bewildered, "Gary, please go pick up your room." She stepped forward into the doorway, "Hi Jack, what can I do for you?"

Jack was watching Gary retreat into the house, "Ryder left his bowling bag at the alley again. I thought I would drop it by."

Karen opened the screen door to accept the bag.

Jack said, "It's kind of heavy, he has two balls in here and what must be a few bricks. Do you just want me to set it inside somewhere?"

"I'm pretty sure I can handle it, Jack," Karen thrust her hand out further while holding the screen door open.

"Ok, Karen," he handed her the bag.

"Thanks, Jack. I'll let him know you brought it by."

Jack held on to the screen door, "Karen is everything ok? You seem a bit distracted. And Gary looks like he was in a fight."

"Everything is fine. Now I need to get back to my kitchen, Jack," Karen smiled, "You have a good day now, bye."

"Bye, Karen." Jack stepped back to let the screen door close, watched Karen shut the main door and heard the dead bolt slam home. He turned and started the short walk home, three doors down.

A couple of hours had passed since returning Ryder's bowling bag and Jack decided to tend to his front yard. He pulled out the grass trimmer after putting the lawn mower back in the shed; he liked to keep his yard green and trimmed to maintain that curb appeal. There was a large flower garden in his front yard, which at this time of year consisted mostly of Tiger Lilies surrounded by quartz rocks. Those deeply pronounced orange petals with the small black spots on the top of three-foot-tall green stalks were in full bloom. Jack took pride in his perennial flower garden; early in the spring, the crocuses were first to come out, followed by the daffodils. Lilies were next, which held until fall, and then it transitioned into mums. All around the edges, mixed amongst the pretty white quartz, were California poppies. Jack never had to plant anything for this garden to produce so splendidly, but he definitely had to keep up on the weeds.

While bent over his rock garden, pulling bindweeds out from between the rocks, Jack heard a car screech to a halt. Without looking, he knew it was Ryder in his dark grey Altima. Ryder always drove too fast and relied on his brakes too much;

every time he pulled into his driveway it was a screeching halt before he hit the garage door.

As soon as he heard the Walkers' screen door slam shut, Jack also heard Ryder yelling into the house, "Gary!"

This was followed by some more unintelligible shouting, which made Jack stand up and look in the direction of the Walkers' home. The next barrage of yelling was easily identifiable as Ryder, "I told you not to leave your damn bike in the driveway! I almost ran it over, you retard!"

Ryder had busted through the door, yelling at Gary. Karen and Haylee both came running out to the front room where Gary had been playing his video game but was now standing, knees shaking. Ryder slapped him with an open hand across his cheek.

Haylee yelled as she turned to run for her room, crying, "No, Daddy!"

Gary muttered under his breath, "Screw you."

"What was that you just said?" Unfortunately it did not get by Ryder's keen ears.

Gary turned, running for the front door; he did not want another beating today. He made it out the screen door, then jumped on his bike and pedaled as hard as he could. The screen had slammed one more time after his escape, so he knew Ryder was coming after him. He heard the running footsteps falling further behind him. Gary did not look back, he just kept pedaling and hoping he could out-run this lunatic.

Ryder started letting up as he watched Gary speed away. He yelled in his direction, "I'll beat your ass when you get home, retard!"

"Really? That's the way you handle a bike left in the driveway?" Ryder turned to see Jack looking at him while pointing a running garden hose at his flowers.

"None of your business, Jack."

"It looked to me like Gary had a black eye and some red swelling on his cheek as he rode by."

"Like I said, stay out of it, Jack!" Ryder's rage was starting to build.

Jack flatly stated, "It is my business as a bystander if you are attacking a minor, Ryder. Whether or not, he is your stepson."

Ryder started strutting across Jack's lawn, heading directly for him. Jack sprayed Ryder with the hose on full blast. This did not faze Ryder; he did not even put a hand up to try and block the spray.

Jack was getting nervous now, "Don't do something stupid, Ryder!"

Arms at his side and fists clenched, Ryder kept marching. Jack repositioned his grip on the hose as Ryder closed to within ten feet of him. He let about a three-foot length of it hang limply by his side from his right hand. When Ryder appeared to be in range, Jack swung his right arm in an arc, using the hose extension like a bull whip. With his left hand, Ryder caught the hose before it hit his face and yanked it hard, pulling Jack directly to him. Using his right fist, he slugged Jack right in the gut with an undercut, lifting Jack's feet up off the ground.

While Jack was bent forward, holding his stomach and coughing, Ryder kneed him right in the nose, which flipped Jack onto his back on his own front lawn. Jack dazedly reached up to feel his nose; blood was seeping out. Ryder reached down; grabbing the hose and letting a three-foot length hang out of his right hand as Jack had done. He started to pull it over his head in an arc, wanting to whip Jack with his own hose. Right as his arm cleared his head in the arc, it was stopped in place by some unseen strong force. The hose ended up continuing the arc, just in a shorter course and struck Ryder on his right thigh. His thigh screamed out in agony. It stung like crazy. Ryder turned to look at the obstruction.

Doug Hamlin stood a full four inches taller than Ryder and he had Ryder's upper arm secured within his right hand. Ryder shook and tried to step sideways, but he could not budge. Doug threw Ryder backwards, against the trunk of a locust tree in Jack's yard. He then grabbed Ryder by the neck, lifting him an inch off the ground, his back pushed against the tree trunk.

Doug said through angry spittle, "You ever touch my boy again, I will snap your neck!" Doug screamed in anger into Ryder's face, squeezing his neck even harder. Ryder went a deep crimson, then began to turn blue.

Jack jumped up, running over and tapping Doug's shoulder, "Hey buddy, you're going to kill him." A couple more seconds went by so, he tapped his shoulder again, "Let up man, it's ok now."

Doug started releasing his hold, and then dropped his arm. Ryder fell to his knees for a second, gasping, then onto all fours, and remained in that position for a minute, gathering his breath. It was silent for a while as everyone took in the situation. Ryder pushed backwards and sat down on the grass, coughing and massaging his neck, not looking at the two that were staring at him.

Doug broke the silence. "Ryder, or whatever your name is, you drop that restraining order tomorrow or there will be some policemen on your door-step the day after."

When Doug turned to leave he saw Gary was straddling his bike in the middle of the street about a block away, watching the action. Doug raised his arm and hand in a hello gesture. It was returned by Gary, who then turned and pedaled casually away on his bike.

To the stranger's back, Jack said, "Thanks, mister."

He had seen this man walking around the neighborhood before but he was unaware of any affiliation he had with the Walkers. The stranger kept walking away, without another word. Jack recouped, went to the spigot to turn off his hose, then went inside. The dead bolt slamming home was audible.

Chapter Thirty

"Where's my damn ball!" Nick Hamlin yelled while rummaging through the front hall closet.

"Probably in the trunk of your car," replied Wanda calmly from the kitchen.

Nick cussed again to himself and slammed the closet door shut. Grabbing his keys out of the bowl next to the front door he made his way to the 1976 Yellow Ford LTD. This was an elite car for the times, with a big motor and featuring a lot of bells and whistles. Upon opening the trunk, he saw the big white bowling bag that Wanda had bought him a few years ago. There was a red smear on the side of the bag that looked like a hand print. Nick always carried a handkerchief. Pulling it out of his pocket he spat a little into it then wiped the smear off of the bowling bag. He placed the kerchief back in his pocket.

Back inside, Nick yelled down the hall towards the boys' bedrooms, "Grab your bowling balls, boys! Heading out in fifteen minutes."

Doug and Harry shared a bedroom and they were racing around looking for their bowling bags and tying on their shoes. They each had their own bowling bag, which contained a ball, a pair of bowling shoes, a glove and some chalk to help the ball slide smoothly off their fingers. These had been gifts to them from Santa Claus the previous year.

Terry had lost his bag and ball a couple of months ago when he called his father a miser in front of his friends at the bar inside the bowling alley. Terry wanted another dollar to play more pinball when Nick told him, "I don't have money for that kind of tomfoolery." Then Nick turned to the bartender and ordered another round of beers for him and his friends.

Terry had looked at his dad, "You're a miser."

At the time, Nick just laughed it off then continued to banter with his friends. They left the bowling alley and were driving north along Lowell Boulevard, headed home. Doug and Harry were talking up a storm but Terry was solemnly sitting in the front passenger seat, aimlessly staring out the window.

Jim Baker Reservoir bordered Lowell for a short distance and when it was at its closest

point to the water, Nick stopped the car.
He popped the trunk, walked to the back
and pulled out Terry's bowling bag. He
took a few steps toward the water then in
an almost discus-hurler motion he turned in
a circle and propelled the bag towards the
reservoir. There was a huge splash then the
bowling bag sat on top of the water for a
minute, like it was going to float, but it
finally subsided and began to sink. After
that, Nick pulled Terry out of the car by his
feet and threw him into the trunk. "This
damn boy always embarrasses me," he kept
muttering to himself all the way home.

"Five minutes, boys!"

"We'll be ready," answered Harry.

Doug and Harry ran out of their
bedroom to the front entryway, with all of
their gear in tow.

"Where's your brother? Never
mind…"   Nick stepped toward the hallway
and yelled, "Terry! C'mon, let's go."

"I don't have a ball, Dad."

Wanda turned to glare at Nick, "What's
he talking about?"

"Sometimes children need to be
punished, Wanda. He'll get it back when he
has proven he is once again worthy."

"C'mon, Terry. You can use a house
ball this one time," said Wanda, who was

standing over by Terry's closed bedroom door.

Terry opened the door, his head held low. He knew it was better to obey than to disobey his father. Sometimes the consequences were harsh.

"That's the sport! Now, let's get going," said Nick.

The Hamlins got a lane immediately and they were busy getting everything situated. Terry walked up to the house ball shelves and found one that was suitable. He did not have his bowling shoes either and since his step-father refused to rent him any, he would have to bowl sock-footed. They always set the board up with a few coin tosses. Harry would roll first this time and Nick would bowl last in each frame.

Nick had been working with Doug and Harry on their bowling stance and approach form. They were learning to throw a curve ball like the professionals. That was for the first ball only, until they gained more control. If they had to throw a second ball in a frame, it would be a straight ball and they would line up their ball and feet with the arrows painted on the floor. Harry started off the first game with a strike.

"All right, champ! That's the way to lead off, Harry," Nick chimed proudly.

They all had a decent game and the scores went in the order of their ages. Harry bowled a 165 which made him happy, being above his average. Doug and Terry bowled just a little higher and Nick threw a 238. Most everyone that bowled at this alley knew or had heard of Nick. He was a well-respected bowler, having won some major tournaments around the city.

"Let's take a five minute break, boys. Anyone want a hot dog and a soda?"

"Oh yeah!" Doug answered cheerfully.

Nick gave Doug a ten-dollar bill and said, "That should be enough for three hot dogs and sodas."

Nick turned, headed to the bar and ordered two beers for himself. He knew the bartender by name; "How you doing, Ray?"

"Pretty good ... you?"

"Hard to beat a day at the bowling alley with your boys."

"Amen, Nick."

They were in the tenth frame of the second game and Harry was right in the mix with his brothers. Only Terry was ahead by five pins. Doug had already finished his game. Terry had resorted to heckling Harry when it was his turn to bowl. Nick did not shush him; he was on beer number four now and was enjoying the revelry. He also wanted Harry to learn about adversity and besides, he was doing a fine job. Each time he would grab his ball from the ball return area there was this glaze of concentration that drifted over his face. It seemed as though he could not see or hear anyone. Hunched over in his stance, he took the three steps and released the ball.

"Strike! Nice shot, Harry," Nick yelled.

Terry replied, "Dang, man."

Harry did not reply or respond in any manner. He turned to grab the ball from the return area, dropped into his stance, took the three steps on his approach and released another perfect roll.

"Strike two!"

Nick, Terry and Doug were intently watching Harry. Terry had stopped heckling because it did not seem to faze Harry, but instead began to encourage him. Harry went through the same repetition and ended his tenth frame in a turkey: three strikes.

Harry fist-pumped the air in celebration, "Yes!"

Nick raised his hand as Harry was returning to the waiting area and Harry slapped him a high five. This really made Harry's emotions swell; his father rarely did that with him.

Now it was Terry's turn to bowl his tenth frame and Doug started heckling him. Terry looked back at Doug, gave him an evil eye and shook his head in disgust.

Nick slapped his leg and started laughing, "If you can't take the medicine, don't dish it out, Terry."

Terry got into his stance and rolled his curve ball down the lane.

"Strike … way to stand up to the pressure, Terry," Nick said.

Terry flipped off Doug with a sneering smile.

"I'm gonna break that thing off and shove it you know where," Doug replied.

Terry stepped up and proceeded to throw a split that was near impossible to turn into a spare. Regardless, that was the end of Terry's come from behind. Harry had beaten his brothers for the first time, along with racking up his highest score. He was elated.

They all took another five-minute break while Nick ran over to the bar area for two more beers.

Ray asked, "Still having a good time, Nick?"

"The best! My youngest, Harry, just beat my other two boys for the first time."

Nick turned without further ado to head back for the third and final game. It was not nearly as close, but just as exciting. Harry ended up beating both of his brothers again, with a 235, which was higher than his previous game. In fact, he almost beat Nick; missed that honor by eleven pins.

Nick high-fived Harry again, "All right, slugger!"

Doug rubbed the top of Harry's head, "Great bowling, Harry!"

Terry just sat down, started to pull on his shoes then put his ball back with the other house balls. Nick was a little disgusted at this display of poor sportsmanship. He guzzled his last beer.

"OK, boys, grab your gear, let's go."

Harry was still living his high. He was talking it up with his father, "Can we go again next Saturday, Dad? I think I can really get the hang of this game!"

Terry stopped and turned to Harry, "Give it up, Harry! You had two lucky games, whoopee!"

Nick looked at Terry, "You know what, Terry, for that outburst, you can come over here and carry both of your brothers' bowling bags to the car!"

They were all quiet the rest of the walk across the parking lot to the big yellow Ford LTD. Nick opened the trunk with his key to put in his bowling bag then handed the keys to Doug, "Open the passenger door for you and Harry."

Terry, struggling with the weight of the two bags, made it to the rear of the car and set them onto the ground. He started to rise when Nick stopped him by grabbing the back of his neck, "What are you doing?"

"I carried them here."

"Pick them up and put them in the trunk!"

Terry could not see his stepdad since he was bent forward. He just heard the seething hatred in his voice. He reached down and grabbed the first bag, Nick let go of his neck, and then he slung the bag into the trunk. Terry bent down, brought up the second bag and placed it next to the other. Once he let go of the handle he felt a hand on his right shoulder spin him around. Now he was facing Nick.

Before Terry knew it, Nick's right fist struck him in the face and he fell backwards into the trunk, on top of the bowling bags. He let out a startled cry. Nick quickly reached in, grabbing Terry by the neck and pushing him down. With fire in his eyes Nick said through clenched teeth, "Why do you embarrass me! That was a disgusting display of unsportsmanlike conduct!"

"Sorry, Dad."

"I am not your dad," Nick then pushed harder against Terry's neck and used his other hand to get Terry in past the bowling bags. He grabbed the trunk lid and slammed it shut, smacking Terry's left elbow as the lid came down.

Doug and Harry were sitting in the front seat. They heard a thump along with a small cry, and then the car rocked back like something heavy was in the trunk. There was a loud, "Ouch," when the trunk was slammed shut. Nick came up to the driver side door and tried to get in, but it was locked.

Harry said, "Oh sorry, Dad," as he reached over to unlock it for him.

Nick dropped in, fired up the Ford and sped home. The ride was silent. Five minutes later they pulled into the driveway. Nick parked the car, turned it off, got out and started heading toward the front door. Harry and Doug looked at each other, shrugged their shoulders and followed their father.

"Harry, get me a beer would ya?" Nick said as he sat down on the couch and turned on the television.

The three of them sat in the front room, watching a Denver Nuggets game. The minimal chatter was only about the game or players. They had watched a whole half before their mother decided to join them in the front room.

"Where's Terry?" Wanda asked.

Nick reached into his pocket pulling out his keys, "Doug, would you go get Terry?"

Wanda retorted, "Damnit, Nick!"

Chapter Thirty-One

"I'll take the lead on this. You guys aren't big enough to knock down the spider webs and move the brush piles," Doug stated as he stopped on top of the berm that descended into a ditch that was five feet deep.

This time of year it was usually half-full with a steady, walking-speed, flow of water. Harry finally made it to the berm. The Hamlin brothers pulled up and stood side by side, looking down at the mucky water lining the bottom of the ditch. Each of them was holding an inner tube float from some old tires that their father had stacked behind the shed. Doug had the largest one.

They were quiet for a minute, thinking about their ride. Terry broke the silence, "There it is. The best water ride in the world!"

"Woo hoo," yelled Harry.

Doug smiled and continued to survey the ditch. It was narrow, with only about four inches of extra space on each side of his tube while he was floating. Every time they rode this ditch there was some new snag or unwanted piece of furniture thrown in that would block their progress. He was the most capable of handling the snags or getting everyone stopped so they could crawl out of the ditch, making their way around the impediment then dropping back into the water.

The ditch did not have a name. Nobody really knew what it was for, besides carrying water from Clear Creek and right back into Clear Creek two miles further downstream. But the Hamlins loved it and it was the perfect cure for a ninety-degree summer day.

Doug pulled the tube up so it was covering his midsection, took three steps back, then ran and jumped forward into the ditch as he yelled, "Yee haw!"

There was a big splash that reached his two brothers. Doug had landed perfectly in the ditch with the tube under him and managed to keep it under control through the shock waves. They were all going to get soaked so his brothers did not care about the back splash and followed his lead. Terry was in the rear.

The first thing Doug always did when they started on their journey was grab a three- or four-foot sturdy stick off the bank. This came in handy, to knock down spider webs in front of them and push obstacles out of the way. Large bushes, tall grass and bends obstructed the visibility ahead and reduced it to a maximum of twenty feet. Sometimes, when the branches and grass leaned over into the ditch, the view would be inches.

A rather long garter snake was the first obstacle to come slithering out of the grass, off the right bank of the ditch and straight into the water. Doug saw it immediately. Pushing his stick out under the water and the snake, he lifted it up and threw the snake back onto the bank. He figured the snake would disappear and his brothers would be none the wiser. *Hopefully Terry doesn't see it. He'll try to catch it and may kill it for no reason.*

Behind him Harry yelled, "Snake!"

This made Doug smile to himself. His brother was courageous when he was around, but seemed to be afraid of his own skin when not.

"Where? I don't see it," Terry asked.

Terry grabbed a clump of grass to slow himself down. He was searching hard but the snake managed to cross over the berm and get out of his sight.

The rest of the float was uneventful in terms of obstacles. It was a nice leisurely ride that produced the desired cool-down with a hint of adventure. They only had to withdraw from the ditch once and walk around the culvert going under Indiana Street.

A few years before they had agreed to float on through the culvert, which was a big mistake. Halfway under the street there was a large rock that each of them got hung up on. Standing to maneuver around the rock produced spiders in their hair and birds dive-bombing them, creating quite the squawking chaos. Once they made it back to the light on the other side there were a few minutes of spider dancing to make certain all of them were arachnid-free.

Near the confluence where the ditch water went back into Clear Creek was where the boys would stop. The creek was too big and swift to float down in an inner tube. Right next to this confluence was an old train yard that was used by Coors brewing company. A lot of times, they would leave their tubes and investigate the train yard. All kinds of things could be found amongst the train cars, including the occasional freight-hopper. Sometimes they would be lying in an open car on top of all their worldly possessions, reading a book. Other times they would be passed out drunk, next to a tipped over bottle.

One time Terry picked up the bottle that was lying sideways next to its owner and took a big swig. Looking at him in disgust, Harry and

Doug let out an, "Eww, that's gross." Then, just as quickly, "What did it taste like?"

Terry never answered, he just let out a big refreshing, "Ahhh."

For some reason, they never ran into any authoritative figure while in the train yards. They came across the occasional hobo but nobody else, which was probably the reason the hobos were there.

Hide and seek was a favorite game of theirs in the yard. There were so many places to hide and the stage constantly changed, since the trains were moved around. Also, the cargo within each boxcar would differ; beer kegs and large wooden barrels were the most common. It was easy to remain hidden amongst the different loads.

Once in a while, they would witness a moving train. The trains would leave or move around the yard at a very slow pace, literally a fast walking speed. This was the most fun when the boys would try their skills at freight-hopping. The hardest part was finding a debris-free section to run across and be able to jump high enough to grab the floor base of an open car and then get your feet up and braced onto the cables and lines underneath the train. Once in this position, it was not too hard to pull yourself up and into the car while also pushing with your feet.

Of course, Harry always had the most difficulty; he could barely do one pull-up. Doug would usually take the lead on being the first into the car, helping Harry get aboard by grabbing his hand and yanking him up. Terry always managed by himself; he was fast and could jump high. The three of them would sit with their feet dangling out the door, daydreaming as they watched the yard pass by.

Terry interrupted the silence, "Maybe, one day we could do this. Go someplace cool, like New York City!"

"Dream on," Doug replied.

Harry asked, "What's in New York City?"

Doug snickered, "Pollution and murderers."

"Oh, come on. Who doesn't want to see New York City? The city that never sleeps. Times Square, the Empire State Building and the Statue of Liberty all spread out along the shores of the Atlantic Ocean."

"I want to go," Harry replied.

Doug looked at the both of them. "Be real. How do you guys plan on eating and drinking? Or are you just going to steal food and whiskey from the hobo's?"

Harry looked to Terry, wondering what the answer could be.

Terry just shook his head, "You're such a buzz-kill. Can't you ever just fantasize or daydream about something you want to do?"

Doug looked back out their front view seat, watching the scenery pass by. "That's a pretend world, like those stupid cartoons you watch and the comic books you read."

Silence ensued for a few minutes. Terry got up and walked around the inside of the empty boxcar.

"It's only pretend if you don't do it," Terry stated loudly. "In fact, there is nothing keeping me here. I may just disappear one day. "

"What about us, Terry?" Harry said. "I know you're mean to us and stuff, but I thought it was just because you liked us."

"Screw you guys!" Terry yelled as he was walking toward Harry, shaking a finger at him. "I could take it or leave it." He poked Harry in his side then smacked him with his open hand on the cheek. Harry looked down and away, tears sharp in his eyes.

Doug stood up and faced Terry, "What the hell was that for?"

"The punk doesn't know when to leave well enough alone."

"Well then, that makes you the punk!" Doug spurted as he tightened his fists and marched toward Terry. Harry was scared and tired of all the fighting. He decided he was just going to head home now, instead of watching another episode of his brothers battling. He thought, if only he had a six pack of beer to make them get along. From where he sat, feet dangling, he pushed himself off the boxcar floor to the ground. He landed gracefully, walking away toward his inner tube, which he would pick up and carry home. The screaming and hollering continued behind him. He didn't even bother looking back.

Harry heard Terry yell, "Don't, Doug, I'm stuck!"

That was louder and seemed to be the voice of terror. Harry turned just in time to see Terry hanging onto the boxcar floor, with one foot dangling over a railroad track and the other looking to be caught in the cables underneath the boxcar. Terry was struggling to try and free himself. Doug walked nonchalantly up to Terry, looking down at him for a minute. He was not trying to help him in any way. Doug spread his arms a little bit then pulled his right leg back and flung it forward, kicking Terry right in the face. Terry's body reacted like a rag doll. With his right foot caught in the cables, he swung out and then his leg caught, which flipped him upside down and brought him back toward the boxcar, but underneath it. His whole body flew underneath the boxcar and landed face-down covering the railroad track with his midsection.

Harry couldn't believe his eyes. The train was slowly creeping closer and Terry was not moving. Doug had dropped down on all fours to look down and see where Terry had fallen. He saw nothing, looking at his younger brother with a confused look and his arms outstretched in the 'what happened' pose. At that very moment, Harry witnessed the most damaging sight he ever would. The train wheel hit Terry in the side and pushed him along sideways for a few seconds until part of his shirt caught under the wheel. A huge spray of red liquid hit the underside of the train and the wheel. It did not affect the train's forward momentum in the least.

Terry's legs remained in the same place while his torso was bounced around under the train, between the two rails.

Chapter Thirty-Two

As with all funerals, it was a sad, humbling affair, and it really bothered Harry that his father had not shed a tear or seemed the least bit mournful. Harry started to wonder if their father had asked Doug to do what he did to Terry. If he had not looked back right when he did, there would be no question in his mind that it was an accident, but that was not the case. Doug kicked Terry right in the face, which sent Terry reeling under the rail car. Had his father and brother conspired to kill Terry?

At least Doug was showing sorrow and, Harry thought, what also seemed to be fear. Doug would look at him with enlarged red-rimmed eyes as if pleading for Harry to speak to him. Harry could not bring himself to listen to or look at Doug directly; he needed time to sort some things out in his head, like what he had seen.

The police had asked him several times to retell the events he remembered, over and over. Harry made sure he did not include the part about him turning around to watch the last fatal seconds. He heard a scream but by the time he turned around it was too late and Doug was nowhere in sight. This was the story the two of them concocted up on the jog home to tell their parents and call the police.

Doug had kept pleading with him, "Harry, it was an accident, I swear! You gotta believe me!"

There were so many times Harry wished he could go back in time and remain oblivious to what he had seen. He loved his brother Doug and the time they spent together; his protector and confidant. But murder … how could he do this to his own stepbrother? Terry had been mean to Harry, but he was that way with everyone. Although he doubted that Terry had tried to help anyone else slide off a cliff. Ever since that day, he had held on to the hope that Terry was going to grab him at the last second. But wasn't that when Doug saved him; the last second? It was hard for him to replay that scene in his head, it was truly terrifying.

Harry reeled into himself, becoming withdrawn, and would not communicate with Doug. He used to sit next to his brother at the dinner table but he chose to take Terry's chair, which was the furthest from Doug. Harry also moved into Terry's old room and would keep the door shut most of the time, never inviting Doug in.

Wanda started to worry about Harry, but was still grieving her eldest son's passing. Most days she was unkempt and would lie around the house, crying, in the robe she had been wearing all week. Lately, Doug had noticed she started drinking more often during the day, while his father was at work. She had talked with a few counselors but this didn't seem to help, it just brought up other issues with her husband and their relationship. Drinking seemed to wash everything away and make life more manageable. After she became a little tipsy, Doug would sometimes sneak over to her bottle with a canteen and embezzle some of the clear liquid that Terry had told him was made from potatoes. He would then head to the tree house with a soda to help him choke down the rather harsh taste. Many times, he would talk to Terry as if he was still alive; crying, laughing, and asking him questions.

Of course, Nick seemed to have perked up with the new family dynamics. His marriage was a little rocky, but he figured that would pass once the grieving ended, which would only take time to heal. In the meantime, his goal was to try to get his sons back into a more collaborative family connection. Doug seemed to be the only one reaching out an olive branch to try and make their strained relationship become fruitful again. Nick had sat down and talked with Harry several times, to try and figure out the sudden change of heart he had for Doug. But he could never get to the meat of it; Harry would clam up and crawl back into his shell. The only time Harry would want to even be seen with or tolerate his surviving brother was when they were bowling. So Nick took them bowling quite regularly.

Harry had developed quite the knack for bowling and would come a little ways out of the shell he created while they were at the alley. Once they finished bowling, though, he would slide into the back seat, staring out the window, and remain silent. He always had a dreamy gaze on his face while he was in this trance. That gaze would appear on Harry's face every time Doug came into sight.

Chapter Thirty-Three

Gary had just sat down on the bike seat as he rode past the big friendly man he had seen a few times and who always waved to him. Each time he felt that there was something strangely familiar about this man, but he could not place it. This time, the man was looking at him more curiously and concerned.

The man seemed like he wanted to say something to him, by raising a finger as he started to speak, so Gary slowed down and stopped his bike in the middle of the street. He knew that Ryder had withdrawn from the chase. Standing on the sidewalk, this behemoth of a man was just about to say something to him when some loud yelling and arguing started back the way Gary had just come.

That stopped the man from speaking as he turned to look in the direction of the disturbance, which was about two blocks away.

He shook his head then waved a goodbye and started jogging down the street towards the noise. Gary did remember seeing Jack out of the corner of his eye while he was pedaling hard. He recognized one of the loud voices as Ryder's, and figured Jack must have said something to make Ryder mad.

Gary was curious as to what the stranger was going to do so he followed behind him and stopped on the other side of the road to watch. He remained at a safe distance to be sure Ryder would not be able to catch him. Ryder was taking it to Jack very handily. Gary was mesmerized by the whole scene. The stranger had slowed down to a brisk walk as he stepped onto Jack's lawn. Ryder reared his arm back, hose in hand, unaware of his new assailant. Gary watched as Ryder's arm was stopped dead by the stranger. The stranger threw him around with ease and it took Jack's begging to make him stop. Gary saw Ryder drop to the ground and almost started cheering; he did pump his fist in the air, but did not want Ryder to know he had witnessed this fight. Especially since Ryder had lost. He was so prideful that he might just kill Gary and Jack before word got around that he was beaten.

Once the fight ended, the stranger caught him watching then just waved his hand high in the air. After Gary responded with the same gesture, he put his head down and started walking back the way he had come.

Gary put his feet back on the pedals and started for Jeremy's home. He was coasting along down a gradual slope, thinking about the stranger, when it dawned on him why the man seemed so familiar. That was the man standing next to his mom while she was pregnant with him, in that picture she kept hidden in the bottom drawer of her dresser. Karen had shown Gary that picture a couple of times to remind him that Ryder was not his father. Gary's smile grew and he thought; *That big man isn't my guardian angel, he's my dad!* He was excited now and stood up on his pedals to pump them harder. Gary had some news to share with Jeremy. He was very impressed with his true father; he had never seen anybody get the better of Ryder.

Dave Olsen was outside, rubbing a soapy sponge over one of their many cars. He held the usual beer can in his free hand. Tonya always stated how talented Dave was: "The tasks that man could accomplish with a single arm, since the other one always holds a beer, are amazing."

Gary pulled up onto their grass and dropped his bike in the middle of the yard next to Jeremy's.

"Hi, Mr. Olsen."

"Why hello there, Gary. How has your day been so far?"

Gary just shrugged his shoulders.

"That's it? Nothing more?"

"Not really." Gary did not want to get into a conversation with Mr. Olsen. Plus, he saw the surprise in the man's eyes when he looked at Gary's face, before turning to washing the car.

Dave had met Ryder once and cared to never do so again; besides, it was none of his business.

"Go on inside. Jeremy's in there somewhere."

Gary smelled peanut butter cookies the second he opened the screen door. He stepped into the kitchen to find Brenda and Tonya rolling out more dough and jabbering away.

"Well, look what the cat drug in, or did you follow your nose from your house looking for the source of the cookie smell?"

Gary smiled, "Hi, Mrs. Olsen. It does smell wonderful."

"Hi Gary," said Brenda.

Gary blushed a little, "Hi, Brenda."

Tonya asked, "We are just about ready to pull out the first tray. Do you want to stick around for three minutes and be our taste-tester?"

"I would love to!" Gary replied as he walked over to pick a chair near Brenda.

Brenda looked at him in a concerned manner, reached her hand out to turn his head a little and get a better look at his eye.

"How did that come about, Gary?"

"Oh, I'm such a klutz, I fell face-first into a door knob."

Tonya interrupted, "Isn't that what happened to you last month?"

"Umm, yeah, it was the same door knob, too."

"Well, you and Jeremy need to spend more time at a gym or outside, instead of on a bean bag in the basement playing video games."

Gary was saved by the bell of Mrs. Olsen's timer announcing that the cookies were ready. She pulled out two big cooking sheets of them. Grabbing a spatula, she scooped up six cookies, placed them on a plate, then handed it to Gary.

"Jeremy is downstairs, run those on down for the both of you."

"Thanks, Mrs. Olsen," Gary smiled at Brenda, who returned more of a worried half-smile.

Gary rushed down the stairs to Jeremy's lair, "Jeremy, you won't believe it!"

Jeremy looked up from the television at Gary with a surprised face, "Oh, hey Gary. You scared me."

"Sorry," Gary handed a cookie to Jeremy then grabbed one himself.

"I see Ryder freshened up your face. Any other bruises?"

"Not really, just a little on my arms and ribs."

"So what is this that I won't believe?"

"My dad kicked Ryder's ass today! Actually, Mr. Peterson had to ask my dad to stop before he killed Ryder!" Gary said loudly with another fist-pump in the air.

Jeremy was listening but still playing a video game.

"You should have seen him. He threw Ryder against a tree and picked him up off the ground with one arm, by his neck. He's so strong and unstoppable that it looked like he was playing with a rag doll. I know it's him. His image matches perfectly with that picture and the little I remember of him."

"What picture?"

"Oh, my mom has a picture of my dad in her dresser. She has shown it to me a few times. I also go in there and take it back to my room sometimes, just to wonder about him. Like why he left. Why he stopped coming to see me."

"That's pretty cool, but why did he wait until now?"

"I don't know. Don't ruin my happiness. Switch this thing over to the two-player version and I'll show you how to get to the next level."

"What?"

"My mom bought me the game, I've been to level six."

"Damn, man. Yes, please show me."

Chapter Thirty-Four

Jack really struggled with the idea but he figured if Ryder was beating Gary that this might shed some more light on the issue. He did not want to cause any more heartache for the boy; however, he also didn't want the boy to end up on a missing persons list or milk carton. Gary was a good, smart kid with a bright demeanor.

"Adams County Sheriff Department, Detective Gomez speaking."

"Hi, I'd like to report an assault."

"OK, is this assault occurring at the moment?"

"No, it ended about thirty minutes ago."

"Can I have your name, sir?"

"Yes, it's Jack. Jack Peterson."

"Who is the victim of said assault?"

"I am."

"Is the assailant still present or in view?"

"No, he walked home. He is a neighbor."

Detective Gomez gathered a little more information then announced to Jack that somebody would be at his doorstep within the hour and that if his assailant returned to call 9-1-1. Jack sat back heavily in his recliner, knowing that now there was no going back to being friendly neighbors on the same bowling team. He adjusted the ice pack on his nose and sighed as he muttered, "Damnit, that's the only time that I ever get out of this house."

Only fifteen minutes had passed when a nondescript tan sedan pulled into his driveway. Two men got out and approached the door. They were dressed in plain clothes; khakis, white shirt and a sport jacket covering a loose tie. Jack pulled open the door before they could knock.

"Jack Peterson?"

"Yes."

The man offered his hand, "I am Detective Gomez and this here is my partner, Detective Singer."

Jack shook their hands, "Nice to meet you."

Gomez asked, "I am assuming that rather broken-looking nose was the true victim in this assault?"

"Yes, I finally got the bleeding stopped."

"Are you sure you don't want to go to the hospital?"

"I'm good. I don't think it's any more crooked than it was before. Just a little more swollen."

"So you said your assailant was a neighbor?"

"Yes, he lives three doors down where that Nissan Altima is parked."

At that moment, Ryder emerged from the house, wearing some kind of uniform. He noticed the two men talking with Jack, looking his direction. Ryder hurriedly walked around to the driver's door, yanked it open, jumped in, then started the car up and took off down the street.

Gomez figured the guy was going to work, due to the way he was dressed. He watched the Altima drive away. He did not want this to turn into a dangerous police chase, "Can you tell me his name?"

"Ryder Walker."

"And what brought about this assault?"

"I overheard something he yelled at his retreating son and confronted him on it."

"May I ask what you heard?"

"He was chasing his son, Gary, down the street and yelled, for verbatim, 'I'll beat your ass when you get home, retard!'"

"Have you ever seen Ryder physically abuse his son?"

"No, but the boy does end up with black eyes, along with cuts and scrapes, quite often."

"Jack, would you like to press charges?"

"Yes, sir. It was a tough decision, but it needs to happen."

Gomez stepped over to Singer; they spoke for a minute and then he returned to Jack. "Detective Singer here is going to take your sworn statement. I am going to contact the home, purely police procedure."

"OK, his wife Karen is a nice lady."

Detective Singer interrupts, "Would you mind doing this someplace more comfortable? Maybe with a chair and table I can fill out this report on."

"Of course, come on in."

Haylee saw Gomez approaching the Walkers' home. "Mommy, there is a strange guy coming to the front door."

"Don't answer it, Haylee, I will be right there."

Karen pulled the door open on the second series of knocking; the screen door was still locked. "Yes?"

"Karen?"

"Yes."

Gomez lifted his coat to show his badge that was attached to his belt, "I am Detective Gomez and we have a neighbor accusing a..." he looked down at his notepad, "... Ryder Walker, of a crime of second-degree assault."

Karen's eyes grew in size and she covered her mouth, not holding back any emotion, "Oh god, what did he do?"

Gomez smiled, "He was involved in an altercation. Your neighbor has a broken nose with a battle story."

"Oh no, who is it? Jack?"

"Karen, the altercation is one thing, but there is something else I'd like to discuss. He was chasing and threatening a boy, Gary, and there is also mention of visible marks on him. Do you know this Gary?"

"Yes, he is my son. His stepfather has been under a lot of stress lately."

"I see. Can you tell me where I can find Ryder?"

"He left for work just a few minutes ago."

"Where might that be?"

"The auto parts store on 64th Avenue, just west of Sheridan."

"When might you expect him home?"

"Around 5:00 PM."

"Thank you, Karen. Have a nice day."

Once the detective had left, Karen toyed with the idea of warning Ryder but she thought better of it. *Maybe this is a sign that all will get better*. She decided to stay out of it and let the chips fall where they may.

Gomez sat on the hood, thinking about the situation, awaiting Singer's return from taking the victim's statement. Karen seemed perplexed about the fight with the neighbor, but not so much Ryder threatening the boy. Gomez cut her interview short; he knew she was not going to say any more than what she had told him. She was definitely shaken, but was it from the neighbor fight or her son being threatened by his stepfather? The suspect had seemed a little rushed while heading for his car, but all he did was yell a threat at his son and break a guy's nose, who may have deserved it. He thought, *If I had a nickel for every time my father threatened me.*

Gomez and Singer pulled up to the auto parts store where Ryder was employed. After talking to the store clerk, they found that he had called in an hour ago to take a personal day. According to the clerk, this was an unusual action for Ryder; he apparently never missed a shift.

"We knew he made us out this morning at Jack's," Gomez paused, "but I didn't think he would run. It's a rather minor crime and he has a family."

"Yep, let's put a sentry at his house and workplace. I don't think we have enough for an APB."

Meanwhile, at the bowling alley, Ryder ordered his first beer at 10:00 AM, just fifteen minutes after he arrived. He'd had such a bad morning that he decided to take the day off work. Those men on Jack's doorstep had to be police and he was not in the mood to talk to them. He thought, *We just had a little fight; it will blow over by tomorrow. Besides, Jack mouthed off to me.*

Ryder rented his own bowling lane. When asked how many games he would like, he told them he would know that once he was finished. He was glad that he had forgotten to take his bowling bag out of the trunk after league night last Wednesday. Ryder bowled a couple of games and then decided to get a couple hot dogs and another beer. It took four beers to put the thought of the policemen at Jack's doorstep aside. Now he was enjoying his day.

He approached the bar. "Hi Ray, can I get another Coors?"

"Sure thing, I see you're by yourself today. Practicing, or did you beat up all your friends?"

"Ha! That's funny, because that is exactly what I did! Make it two, Ray."

Double-fisted with Coors, Ryder bowled another game then returned to the bar. It was nearly 10:00 PM; Ryder had been drinking for twelve hours and was too drunk to stand. He managed to shuffle down to where his bowling bag stood open next to the lane he had bowled. At one point, he had to crawl because the steps were too steep. Ray was giggling to himself as he watched Ryder crawl, fall, bounce off chairs, and finally take a face-first digger on the carpeted entry way, trying to escape the bowling alley. He watched him through the glass doors make it to his car and speed away, leaving his bowling bag where he had fallen.

Hank was manning the last of the customers at the drive-thru window while Tom was mopping and cleaning the floors in preparation to close for the night. The last order had been received and Hank had it all assembled, waiting for the driver. He gave the customer a couple of minutes, figuring he was counting change or something. Then a loud continuous honk blared out from the Nissan Altima sitting in the drive-thru lane, startling both of them.

Hank tried to raise the customer on the speaker but all that could be heard was the horn. They both jogged out to the car. Hank opened the door and Tom knelt down to look at the man, pulling his head back off the steering wheel to stop the horn.

"He's got a pulse," Tom said.

"Look at the beer cans, he's passed out drunk."

"You better call the cops, Hank."

"Tom, it's almost closing time and I got a date with Darlene tonight!"

"So? What's that got to do with anything?"

"If we call the cops, we'll be sitting here for who knows how long, while they try and sort it out. That could take hours, man."

"True. I'm meeting some friends myself, in thirty minutes."

"C'mon, let's just push his car over there in that empty parking spot, turn off the lights and lock him in the car."

"We can't leave his keys in there with him, he may wake up and drive drunk."

"Look, I don't want to sit around here and wait for him to wake up, either. I'll put them under the floor mat. He'll only search there, once he's sober enough."

Chapter Thirty-Five

Jesse was not having much luck in figuring out how to handle this mess with the supposedly abusive father. The family seemed to embrace Ryder enough to stick together and stave off any allegations of abuse. He had to speak with John again; maybe one of his out of the box ideas was what he needed. They were unusual at times but they generally got the job done.

Jesse called John to see if he was available one afternoon to help sort through another issue he was having. This afternoon, John would be working on his Bronco after he got home from work around 4:00 PM.

He hung around most of the day at home with his mom and performed a multitude of chores. Mowed the lawn and weeded the garden, just trying to pass the time until John got home from work. He figured he would be doing this on a weekly basis, even after he moved in with Raven. Becky still relied on a cane to fully maintain her balance.

Jesse showed up at John's house a little after 4:00 PM. He decided to ride his bike over to John's, since he had a case of Coors Banquet beer under his arm. Too many people he knew ended up with DUIs from drinking and driving and he paid heed to their horror stories.

The garage door was not open so he stepped up to the porch and knocked on the door. He knew their doorbell had been ripped out by his father, who hated such things and it did not work. The funny thing about it was the two wires were hanging outside and anyone could grab them and touch them together to make the doorbell chime. Through the screen door; he could see John's father, Kevin, sitting in his Lazy Boy chair with a beer in his hand, watching the Colorado Rockies game. Kevin looked over and saw it was Jesse, and just raised his head in acknowledgement and grunted. Jesse knew that this was his cue to come inside.

"Hi, Mr. Rodney. John around?"

Kevin looked in the direction of the kitchen, where there was a door that opened into the garage. Then he nodded his head in that direction and made the same guttural noise. This meant John was in the garage. Jesse made his way through the kitchen and opened the garage door.

"Hey, Jesse. Right on with the beer, my dad got on my ass last night about drinking all of his."

Jesse shook John's proffered hand, "Hey, John. Yeah, I felt like swigging a few tonight. Raven's out with her mom shopping and I need to bounce something off of you."

"I hope it's not another boomerang!"

Jesse laughed, "Nothing quite so soft."

When they were in fifth grade, Jesse's dad got him a boomerang. He and John were in the park, trying to figure out how to throw it correctly. Jesse whipped it hard overhand and the device twisted and flipped through the air and started banking in a half-moon, right back toward them. John went to catch the boomerang but he missed and it pelted him right in the chest.

"Well, crack me a beer and let me grab my wrenches, then we can get started." John wasn't good at listening if you would just sit down and talk face-to-face in the normal sense. He would get bored and start spacing out or cracking jokes. However, he was a great listener if he had something to work on with his hands. Since John was an auto mechanic, that generally meant he would work on a car. Lots of times, he would pace back and forth with his head down, letting the words sink in.

Jesse started relaying the story to John on what happened at the auto parts store. How Ryder helped him solve his misfiring issue and seemed like a nice enough guy, until the end of their conversation. Jesse was the only one talking, but he knew John was catching every word.

"So a couple days after I went to his store, he showed up in Mr. Romans' lot before I got there. I guess he wanted to let me know that he knew where to find me, if he had to."

John finally spoke, "What do you mean?"

"Well, once he saw me, he rolled down the window telling me he knew where I worked then gave me the bird and took off."

At this point, John crawled out from underneath the Bronco to grab another beer. He took a couple of sips and was pacing for a few. Once in a while he would look at Jesse in incredulous disbelief, and shake his head.

All of a sudden the door that went from the garage to the kitchen burst open and Kevin stepped into the garage. Jesse halted at this point.

"Don't mind me, boys, just grabbing a cold one," Kevin said.

By the way he was walking it was obvious Kevin had quite a head start on them. Jesse continued with the story and in the short time he was in the garage, Kevin must have absorbed enough of it to understand what and who he was talking about.

Kevin stopped on his way back to the kitchen door and looked over at Jesse and listened to his story for a minute longer. Then he asked, "Are you talking about that twerp Ryder that works at the auto parts store on 64th Avenue?"

Jesse thought, *Twerp*. Ryder was kind of a big dude but then John's father was an arm-wrestler at one time in his life and he stood about as tall as he was wide.

Kevin cracked his beer, standing on the step over by the kitchen entrance, "I still feel bad that I talked his brother Doug out of beating him to a pulp and taking back his wife."

"Brother?" Jesse's head came up, looking at Mr. Rodney for more information.

"Yeah. Ryder Walker's real name is Harry Hamlin. He changed it when he was just eighteen years old. He decided he wanted to get away from his dysfunctional family and become a magician, of all things. Moved to Vegas and everything. We went on a road trip to see him at one of his shows, but by then he was already working as a dealer in a casino," Kevin paused and looked at both John and Jesse staring at him in misbelief then continued, "Doug would have gone to jail for a while if I didn't talk him out of it. He has a couple of assault charges. I saw one of the assaults. That is a guy you do not want to piss off."

That meant a lot, coming from Mr. Rodney.

"Now wait a second, Mr. Rodney. You are saying that Doug Hamlin is Ryder's brother, correct?"

"Yeah, his very wife, Karen, doesn't even know that they are brothers. Same mom and dad, true full-blooded brothers. For some reason, that is the ancient Hamlin secret," Kevin slammed the rest of his beer and started walking back to the garage refrigerator, "I'm not sure if their parents were embarrassed by Ryder or if Ryder was trying to separate himself from being a Hamlin."

It was so quiet in the garage when Kevin stopped speaking you could hear a pin drop. He threw his empty into the trash can that said 'cans only' and pulled another beer from the refrigerator.

"Hell, I should know. I grew up with the Hamlin brothers. Doug was in my high school class. Ryder, or Harry as I still remember him, is a couple of years younger. They had an older step-brother named Terry, but he died in a freaky accident involving a train, not long before I met them."

Now it was John's turn to raid the beer stash. He pulled out two and tossed one to Jesse.

Kevin continued, "Harry never talked about it, not even a word. Doug would at times, but every time he would start to bring it up, Harry would leave the room. I used to go to Davies Locker bar to visit Doug once a week, but he is just a useless lush now and is very hard to speak with."

Chapter Thirty-Six

Ryder woke up with a fierce headache and a jarring pain in his side. He covered his eyes with a hand due to the bright light shining through the windshield. Lifting himself up off the gear shift console relieved the pain in his side. Noticing there were no other cars in the parking lot, he looked straight ahead for the source of the light. Just ten feet away was a big fat lit-up yellow 'M' with a red bottom, denoting the name of the establishment. It was dark out and the streets were abandoned. He felt around the ignition, then the seats, to find his keys on the floor-board in a lump under the mat.

Grabbing the door handle, he stepped outside to relieve himself. Then got back into the car and headed for home. The house was dark when he pulled into the driveway to park. Anxious to climb into bed, he stumbled to the door, fumbled for his keys and finally found the door latch. Not more than two minutes after he shut the door, he was in the kitchen raiding the refrigerator when there were some lights shining through the front window. Then there was pounding on the door.

"Open up, Adams County Sheriff's Department!"

Detectives Gomez and Singer decided to take first watch at 5:00 AM. It was generally a nice quiet time of morning and from experience they knew this was the time criminals generally returned to the scene.

"Ah, shit!" Yesterday's events came back to Ryder.

He opened the door and cooperated with the police. While a gun was trained on him, they made him kneel down on the floor and put his hands behind his back. Another officer hand cuffed him and asked Ryder to rise. The first officer put his gun away and started reading Ryder his Miranda rights.

Gomez asked, "Do you understand these rights, Ryder?"

"Yeah, yeah."

Haylee was the only one that came out to see what all the commotion was. "Daddy!"

"Don't worry, darling. Everything is OK. When your mother gets up, tell her Adams County Sheriff."

Haylee asked, "OK, did you kill him?"

Gomez and Singer both looked at each other. That statement seemed a little definitive. Gomez turned and knelt in front of Haylee, "Who was he going to kill?"

Ryder blurted out, "Now you know better than that, baby doll. Daddy would never kill anybody."

Gomez waved his hand at Singer, "Get him out of here!"

"Don't say anything, honey!"

The second Singer and Ryder stepped onto the Walkers' porch they both noticed a big brown diesel truck idling near the sidewalk and a man standing halfway up the walkway, holding a gallon of milk and a flat of eggs.

"You son of a bitch! It was you that ratted me out! You just wait, you'll get yours, punk!"

Singer tightened his hand on Ryder's upper arm, "Do you really think that this is a good time to make threats towards somebody? You know that I can hear you, right?"

Jesse replied, "Wasn't me, Ryder."

Singer smiled, "Hey, Jesse?"

Singer continued walking Ryder over to the tan sedan, locking him in the back seat. Once he shut the door, he turned and leaned across the top of the car, looking back toward Jesse.

"Hi, Detective Singer." Jesse continued up the walk to finish the delivery. Once he shut the lid he heard the front door to the house close and a familiar voice behind him.

"Well, I'll be. How you doing, Jesse?"

Jesse turned to see Gomez and shook his hand, "I'm good, Detective Gomez. Can you tell me what happened here?"

"Well, just the facts. That guy is accused of beating up his neighbor; just accused mind you. He has his own battle wounds, too."

"Understood. Was everyone else inside OK?"

"Now why would you ask that? I get the feeling that again you know something that I should?"

"I'm not holding out, Detective Gomez. I just want to make sure that Karen and Haylee are all right."

Jesse looked at the front window to see Haylee holding a stuffed animal and waving at him. He waved back, and then looked to Gomez.

"It seems your customers really do care about you, Jesse. I'm sure you still have my card. Call me if you can think of anything."

As Gomez approached the car Singer said, "When Jack told his story, it seemed pretty one-sided. But did you see the bruising on that guy's neck?"

"I did, and was thinking the same thing. Regardless, let's run him down to the station and hear his side of the story."

Singer said, "We'll need to fill him up with coffee before he'll be any use to us."

Back at the station, Gomez determined that Ryder was in no condition to be questioned. He opened up a cell with a bed at the Sheriff's Department, letting Ryder sleep off his drink. There was a desk near the cell that he could use to catch up on his paperwork. Karen had contacted him already, asking when she could come pick up Ryder. He explained that he needed to question her husband first and that he was currently sleeping. A couple of hours later, he heard Ryder starting to stir back to life. He watched as the man sat up on his bed, rubbing his head.

Gomez asked, "Coffee?"

"Please."

He returned shortly after, "We only have black here. The department is too cheap to spring for cream and sugar."

Ryder held out his hand, "Thanks."

"Do you know why you are here?"

"Yes."

"How'd those marks on your neck come about?"

"Doug did that to me while Jack and I were arguing."

"Doug?"

"Yeah, Doug Hamlin."

"Do you know where I can find this Doug Hamlin?"

"At one of the three bars in Shaw Heights."

Gomez wrote the information down; he would have to talk with Doug at some point to conclude this investigation. Now he wondered why Ryder was chasing his boy and what was said. Also, why had Jesse shown such an interest? There seemed to be a piece missing.

"Can I ask why you were chasing your son?"

"Stepson. It's a family matter and some punishment was in order."

"Punishment? "

"The boy deserved to be grounded and maybe even a spanking for what he did."

"Is that all?"

Ryder leaned back on the cot, staring at Gomez. "Yep."

"I was told that you wanted to beat the retard's ass when he got home."

This got Ryder's attention. He sat back up, "That was just words said in the heat of passion. I never would have done that."

"Ryder, we take threats like this very seriously."

"I understand, I'm sorry. The boy got under my skin, but you have to believe I would not have raised a hand to him."

Gomez thought he seemed sincere but he needed to pull Karen in to get a deeper understanding of the family dynamics. He called her back. She answered immediately and agreed to come down to the station. Gomez told her he just needed to clear up a couple of things and then he would release Ryder into her custody. In less than ten minutes, she was buzzed in to the back room where Gomez was sitting and Ryder was being detained. Her hair was still a little unkempt and with the redness of her eyes and cheeks he could tell she had been recently crying.

"Karen, the punishments at home; do they ever get out of hand? Maybe a black eye or something like that?"

She was surprised by this question. Looking to Ryder she noticed he was returning her stare. "No, of course not. Nothing like that."

"Jack said that Gary had a prominent black eye when he rode by on his bike."

"Oh, that," she hesitated a little longer than Gomez cared for. "That's because he is a growing teenage boy. He is very klutzy at times."

"Ryder here told me that some guy named Doug…" Gomez looked down at his pad again, "… Hamlin attacked him while he and Jack were arguing. Do you know this Doug Hamlin?"

Karen looked very surprised, "Umm, yes." A little reluctantly she added, "That is Gary's biological father."

Gomez smiled and shook his head, "Do you know why Jack would leave this part of the story out?"

Karen's heart started beating a little harder; *Since Doug is back, should I tell the truth? He would certainly protect us from Ryder.* But she just couldn't do it yet; she feared Doug would let her down again, or have a relapse with the alcohol.

"No, no I don't."

Again, Gomez thought she was deriving her answers on the fly and they were not fully truthful. He was good at reading people, especially people under duress. Sometimes when the culprit was seen locked inside a cell, the victim would become more truthful and open up. He was sure something was going on here, but Karen had shown that she was not going to release that information at this time.

Gomez casually walked over to the cell door, watching Karen as he did so. She watched him put the key into the lock and then she dropped her head. Gomez thought, *As if she blames herself for failing again.*

Gomez handed a piece of paper to Ryder, "This is not the end of this situation. Here is your court summons; you will still stand in front

of a judge on the assault charge." He
turned to Karen, "And Karen, I am
releasing Ryder into your custody. I do not
consider him a flight risk but understand, if
he flees, you are responsible for helping
with his return."

Chapter Thirty-Seven

It only took ten minutes for Gomez to find everything he needed to know about Doug Hamlin. According to his involvement with law enforcement, he should be considered the town drunk. Doug had four outstanding prior offenses that were never handled to completion. He had failed to appear on two court appearances, and he failed to finish attending a series of AA meetings that were part of a drunk and disorderly charge he received. An FTA was serious. Also, many years ago, he had two assault charges that stuck. Any of these other prior offenses could send him away for a long time. Gomez noted Doug's last known address, grabbed his coat and walked down the hallway toward Singer's office.

Singer was kicked back in his chair, looking up as he threw a stress ball at the ceiling. It would bounce off and come shooting back at him, he would then catch it and toss it right back at the ceiling. He was oblivious to his surroundings when he did this. Gomez knew that this was how his partner thought things through and he did not want to startle him, so he cleared his throat.

"Oh, hey Gomez."

"You want to help me on an arrest?"

Singer stood up, grabbing his coat, "Sure, I need some time away to think about this, anyhow."

They strolled silently together out to the car, Gomez carrying a folder. He handed it to Singer, "Here's the guy we are looking for. He is involved with that assault by Ryder, on that guy Jack."

"What?"

"Those marks you saw on his neck. Ryder said those were caused by this guy, Doug Hamlin."

"OK."

"Now, here is the interesting part of the story. Doug Hamlin is the biological father of Gary; the same boy that Ryder was chasing and threatening." Gomez let that sit in the air for a second then finished, "Furthermore, Doug has had a restraining order placed against him from seeing his boy for the last seven years. It doesn't say why."

Singer shook his head in disbelief, "What a strange world."

They pulled the tan sedan into the parking lot of the apartment complex where Doug lived. The plain-clothed detectives were not an out-of-the-ordinary sight in this complex. It seemed like every week a different law enforcement agency would show up. They were glad to see he was on the first floor. Gomez stepped up and pounded on the door, "Adams County Sheriff, we'd like to speak with Doug Hamlin."

Doug's heart skipped a beat. The only thing scarier to him than dying was going to jail and having his freedom taken away. Being on the bottom floor, he could run out his back door, but then what? Where would he go? Besides, he was pretty sure that this was about the fight in that old man's front yard.

Doug pulled the door open and in a deep baritone asked, "What's this about?"

Gomez and Singer stepped back instinctively. They were both impressed how this man filled out the whole door frame and had to duck under the header to look out. Doug Hamlin turned out to be a much bigger man than they had ever dealt with. Singer looked down at the rap sheet again, according to this Doug was six inches over six feet tall and a sturdy 312 pounds.

"Uh, Mr. Hamlin, I am Detective Gomez and this is my partner, Detective Singer."

Doug showed no emotion, he just nodded his head.

"We'd like to ask you a few questions about an altercation you were said to participate in two days ago; last Monday."

Doug started to close the door, "I don't feel like talking about that."

Gomez stuck his foot at the base of the door to keep it from shutting, "Look, we got enough to arrest you and put you away for a long time, just on priors."

The second Gomez finished that sentence, the door flew open and he was off his feet, floating in the air thanks to one massive hand that gripped the front of his jacket, shirt and tie. Gomez grabbed the forearm that was suspending him so he would not choke.

Singer pulled a stun gun, pointing it at Doug's chest, "Put him down and step back."

Gomez yelled, "Shoot him!"

Singer let it fly and it hit Doug right above the stomach. Stun guns were still not very accurate. This just made the walking giant madder. He growled menacingly, tossed Gomez toward the dumpster, which he landed in without even hitting the sides, and then started toward Singer, who had turned up the stun charge to full blast, to no avail. Singer dropped the stun gun and was reaching for his service revolver when a hand clamped down on his shoulder and squeezed so hard that his arm became paralyzed with pain. As he was being forced lower to kneel, Singer watched Gomez climb out of the garbage dumpster clumsily and fall to the ground in front of it.

Gomez yelled at Doug's back, "Doug, we know Gary is your son and just want to help!"

Singer felt the hand start to loosen its grip.

"How can you help?"

"I can get the restraining order lifted. There is no reasoning behind it."

Doug completely let go of Singer, turning toward Gomez, "You better not be lying to me. I don't like people that lie."

"Believe me, I don't want to make you mad," Gomez said as he started to get up off the ground and brush the dirt off his jacket. "Now the only thing is, we need to take you to the station for a statement about your involvement with the altercation."

"Arrrgghh, you lied!" Doug yelled as he plummeted his fist and forearm down onto the top of the tan sedan. It caved in a couple of inches, with a thundering *boom*.

Gomez raised his hands in a stop gesture, "No, no, now hold on. You need to hear me out."

Doug relented again. Singer ran around to the other side of the car to distance himself from

this giant and pulled out the radio to
request back-up if it got out of hand one
more time.

"Look, you have a few priors where the
terms were not completely fulfilled. In the
light of things they are pretty minor,"
Gomez paused, watching Doug, knowing
he had hit a soft spot, "but to get all of this
stuff corrected on your record, so then you
can start over clean and even file for partial
custody, you need to come with us
willingly."

"How much time in the slammer?"

"I don't see more than a week, with
some promises and butt-kissing."

Doug paced around for a minute,
thinking about his options. It seemed he
was more afraid of losing Gary forever than
going to jail for a short time. He relented,
letting his shoulders relax.

"OK," Doug pointed a finger at Gomez,
"if you are lying to me, we will be having a
talk when I get out."

"Trust me, I do not want that to
happen."

"Do you mind if I turn off my stove
and lock the door?"

"Not at all, Detective Singer will help
you out." This was more of an assurance
that Doug would not run or barricade
himself inside. Although Gomez was not

sure they would be able to stop that from happening if he so chose.

Singer looked at him while raising a questioning eyebrow, "Why me?"

Chapter Thirty-Eight

It was the first Sunday that Raven and Jesse got
to wake up next to each other. They slept in
past their usual wake-up times. When Raven
opened her eyes, she noticed Jesse was lying
awake, staring at her.

He smiled, "Pancakes?"

"That sounds marvelous."

They made their way to the kitchen.
Jesse started the coffee and Raven pulled
out a chair to sit. She was quiet for a
minute, looking out their kitchen window,
thinking on where to put the bird feeder
and how she would like to improve the
view with some colorful flowers. Jesse,
meanwhile, was banging up a storm;
whisking batter mix, placing pans on the
stove.

"You want an over-easy egg on top?" Jesse preferred a yolk as runny as syrup on pancakes.

Raven not so much, "No, you can put mine on the side."

Jesse placed the syrup, as well as some forks and napkins, on the table. Giving Raven a kiss on the forehead then stepping back over to the stove, he asked, "What's on your mind?"

"Jesse, I have to ask," she looked over at him while he was busy flipping a pancake, "have you shown that note Haylee left you to Gomez?"

"No, I haven't. I was still trying to determine if it was unjust."

"You need to show it to him."

"OK, I'll call him tomorrow."

"Nope, not tomorrow, today, and I am going with you."

He developed a small smirk, "Don't you trust me?"

She smiled, "Of course I do. It will be fun and then I'll let you buy me lunch afterwards."

Jesse called Gomez and he said it was his day off, but agreed to meet them for lunch at Los Arcos. Raven was on board, she enjoyed their chile rellenos.

Gomez was already seated in a booth with a margarita in hand when they arrived. He was in a jovial mood. They shook hands and carried on with some light banter about the local sports teams. The waitress took their orders. Jesse and Raven stuck with ice tea.

Gomez asked, "So, why do I have the pleasure of seeing you again?"

Jesse started, "Well..."

Gomez interrupted, smiling at Raven, "I'm not talking about your ugly mug. Nice to see you again, Raven."

Raven blushed lightly, "Thank you, Mr. Gomez."

"Gomez, please. Just call me Gomez. I prefer that to my first name," he paused to take a sip of his margarita, "and no, I will not reveal that information at this time."

Raven smiled at Gomez, "Now you sound like Jesse." That got the three of them laughing.

"Ok, so seriously, why am I here?"

Jesse reached into his back pocket and started unfolding a piece of yellow construction paper.

Gomez asked, "What's with you storing things in your back pocket?"

Jesse didn't reply. He continued opening the paper, then started smoothing it out on the table with his forearm.

"Is this another note? From a milk box?"

"Yes, it is, from the Walkers' milk box, to be exact."

Gomez did not show any shock or emotion, "I knew something was wrong when we met on the porch."

Raven said, "He is a little hard headed, but he is here now."

"Well, I'm glad your better half has a brain. You need to involve me sooner with these notes you get."

Jesse replied, "Well, when I met the guy at his work he seemed nice enough. Plus it is a six-year-old girl revealing this story. I just didn't want the guy to be put under the microscope for some exaggerated events."

Gomez asked, "You went to his workplace?"

"Well, yeah."

"You are not a law enforcement officer, Jesse. These matters can become very dangerous. You remember the Carr sisters, right?"

"I do, point taken. Sorry."

"OK, well on this note," Gomez smiled, "or because of this note, I need to call Singer. We now have an interview tomorrow morning."

The booth was quiet for a minute. Gomez smiled at Raven and then stood, offering his hand to Jesse. "Thanks for coming forward, oh, and thanks for lunch."

Chapter Thirty-Nine

Gomez called Singer into his office.

"So that Ryder guy we arrested for assault. It seems Ryder Walker is an alias."

"OK."

"Check out his real name."

"Isn't that the last name of his assailant that we also arrested?"

"I think there is more to this than we thought."

"How about we take a trip to County and talk with Doug a little more?"

"You're assuming he will want to see us."

It had been raining steadily and due to the dent Doug put in the top of Gomez's sedan, the window would not roll up all the way, allowing water to drive inside, splashing the passenger seat. Singer had been riding in the back seat with the amount of rain that had been saturating the area.

Gomez smiled, sticking his hand out, "Hey Doug, thanks for seeing us."

Doug shook the hand, "I don't have much on my plate at the moment."

"We'd like to ask you a few questions about the guy you pulled off of Jack."

Doug snickered, "Ha! What a piece of work he is. Ruined my whole damn life."

"What do you mean?"

Doug put his thick arms on the table and rested his face in his hands, "He's my brother, and Gary's uncle."

Gomez and Singer exchanged looks but remained quiet, hoping Doug would elaborate.

"Our mother had been married previously to an army vet that was killed in action overseas. She had a son by him, Terry. She met our dad not much later. I believe Terry was just two. Anyways, our father never took much to Terry. Didn't consider him part of the family. He was rough with him and flat-out mean. Terry had a heavy heart because of this and would lash out at Harry and me. Thing is, I could man-handle Terry, so I was always protecting Harry. This one time, Terry even tried to kill him, letting him fall off a cliff while throwing pine cones at his face." Doug paused for a second, taking a swig of water. "One day, we were playing in the train yards by Coors and Terry was killed by accident. Harry has always blamed me for that. He became reclusive and didn't want anything to do with me, which was really hard on the family. Once he was of age, Harry changed his name and moved to Las Vegas. Pursuing some stage act as a magician, my mother told me. Then he came back after Dad had passed and acted like he wanted to make amends, but instead he stole my wife and kid. The rest is my fault; I started drinking and didn't stop for seven years, until two months ago."

Doug looked to the detectives for any reaction.

Gomez broke the silence. "Wow, that is quite the family story." Singer just nodded his head in agreement. They were quiet for a minute, just letting the story sink in.

Doug chuckled, "Not your typical family."

Gomez looked at Doug, "Congratulations on quitting the alcohol."

"Thanks, Detective. Anyways, now you have some background on him and the reason I have babbled on for the last five minutes is because I think he is beating my boy, Gary."

That got both the detectives' attention.

Gomez followed up, "What leads you to that conclusion?"

"My boy is not klutzy, he doesn't play sports anymore, but was quite athletic when he did. He keeps developing bruises, scrapes and black eyes. Also, he is afraid of his father."

Gomez asked, "How do you know this? I thought you had a restraining order against seeing him?"

"From a fifty foot distance and I don't believe I have violated that condition. Let's just say I have been conducting my own stakeouts from afar."

"Do you happen to know a certain Jesse Hardner?"

"Can't say I've ever heard that name."

"Have you seen your brother physically abuse anybody around the house?"

"Nope, just his neighbor."

"All right, Mr. Hamlin. I think we have heard enough. Thanks for meeting with us today and for being so candid. We'll be in touch."

When Gomez went to shake Doug's hand, it reminded him of being a child; his hand was completely engulfed and wrapped inside Doug's.

Chapter Forty

The house was restless as Karen was busy getting breakfast made for the family. Haylee was talking up a storm at the kitchen table while preparing the eggs for scrambling with a whisk. Ryder woke up a little late and was behind schedule with his daily routine, which made him even grouchier. He was in the bedroom getting dressed for work when there was a knock at the door. Karen was worried and nervous about Gary; he had called last evening to ask if he could stay the night at Jeremy's house. She told him that was fine but to be home for breakfast. He had not shown up yet but she knew he was probably waiting for Ryder to leave for work. However, the knock made her nervous, hoping it was not bad news regarding Gary.

Wiping her hands on a kitchen towel, she made her way to the peep hole. On the porch was the same man that had arrested Ryder. She reluctantly opened the door, "Hi, how may I help you?"

"Hi, Karen." Gomez looked down at his notebook, "Detective Singer and I were wondering if we could have a word with Ryder this morning?"

"Um, he is getting ready for work. Let me ask him."

Leaving the detectives on the porch, she shut the door and walked back to the master bedroom. The door was open and Ryder was putting on his shirt, the bruising from the confrontation with Doug still visible.

Upon seeing her, Ryder asked, "Who's at the door at this time of day?"

"Detective Gomez and I am assuming his partner."

Disgusted, Ryder looked up at Karen. "What do they want?"

"They said, just to talk. I left them on the front porch."

Ryder finished putting his shoes on and sat on the edge of the bed for a minute contemplating his options. He thought about running out the back door, but that would just admit he had guilt for something.

"All right, tell them I will meet them on the porch in a couple minutes. Do not let them in."

Back at the front door, "He'll be right with you, detectives."

"Karen, do you mind if we do this inside?"

She repeated, "He'll be right with you, detectives."

Gomez and Singer chose a couple chairs to sit in on the front porch. They were quiet, awaiting their interviewee. The two of them had already discussed their tactic and wanted to be able to hear any escape attempt or argument that occurred. It was a nice quiet neighborhood with not much traffic at this time. Finally, the door opened back up and out stepped Ryder. Karen was standing behind the door, getting ready to push it closed.

Gomez looked at Karen. "We would also like you to join the conversation."

Hesitantly, Karen turned back, stepped out onto the porch and pulled the door shut from the outside. She was a bit miffed; Haylee was sitting in her chair whisking the eggs, waiting for breakfast. Also, she was pretty sure Gary was watching the house, waiting for Ryder to leave before coming home.

Both Gomez and Singer had risen out of their chairs and indicated they would like Ryder and Karen to sit. Singer stepped over behind the Walkers, who were facing Gomez.

Gomez looked directly at Ryder, "I'm going to be frank with you, Ryder. It seems there is a growing accusation that you beat your stepson, Gary."

Ryder had an aura of confidence about him that made the detectives think he could handle himself quite sufficiently in a brawl. That was their reasoning for the scene they had sculpted. Singer had his Taser in a handy position, along with a set of handcuffs. They hoped that he did not possess the strength of his brother. Ryder looked to the right; Singer knew it was to gauge where he was standing.

Ryder shook his head in denial, "That's a false statement, Detective."

Gomez did not say anything, he just held eye contact with the accused. He had noticed that Karen twitched a little bit when he said the word 'beat'. Her eyes were a little wider and she watched Ryder's mannerisms. Gomez bet she was wondering if he was going to sit there and take it or fight his way out. She was the one they were hoping would crack, since she seemed like a loving and caring mother.

Gomez pulled a bright yellow piece of paper out of the folder he was holding, "Can you explain this note left in your milk box?"

The yellow piece of construction paper was wrapped in plastic, as if it was being held for evidence. It was easily identified as a young child's writing as well as spelling, written in black crayon.

"Look, detectives, yes, my stepson and I have arguments at times, for Christ sake he is a teenager. But I would never 'beat' him," Ryder used his fingers to quote the words, "Any bruise or black eye he has was done by his own hand. He is rather klutzy."

Gomez looked at Singer, then back over to Karen, "Have you seen any suspicious behavior with your son and this man?"

"No, Ryder does not raise a hand to our children. Any markings are purely coincidental."

"Ok then, well I guess we can ignore this note and chalk this up to a misunderstanding. Sorry to waste your time or cause any more distress."

Finally, Karen spoke up, "Can I ask what has happened to the man that attacked Ryder?"

Gomez smiled, pointing at Ryder, "You mean Gary's dad and this guy's brother, Doug? We arrested him, he's in county jail."

Karen looked like she had just been hit by a steam roller. Her face contorted, she stood up like something filthy was at her feet, and kept looking at Ryder in disbelief, hoping for an explanation. A couple of times, Gomez thought she was about to speak, but then she would clam back up. She would start to open her mouth then shake her head. Finally, she had enough and screamed, "Oh my god!" Then turned and ran into the house.

"She seems to be a little upset, Ryder. Sorry to leave you with that."

Ryder had his head down and was trying to hold in his rage, "Good-bye, Detectives."

Gomez and Singer left without another peep. Ryder sat outside until he saw them turn the corner at the end of the block. He got up and stepped inside. Karen was standing in the kitchen, shaking, trying to mix herself a drink. It was a very stiff drink, only an ice cube accompanying a generous portion of vodka.

"Mommy, aren't we going to make scrambled eggs and toast?"

Karen started shaking more as she took a drink from her glass, not saying a word, just staring at Ryder.

"Haylee, did you leave the milk man a note?"

Haylee looked surprised and scared, "Yes, Daddy."

Ryder yelled, "Damnit, why would you write that, Haylee? You could have gotten Daddy into big trouble!"

The little girl started crying and running for her room, "I'm sorry, Daddy."

"What did you tell the damn milk man, Karen?"

"Nothing, I swear."

Out of the blue, Ryder smacked her with an open hand. Karen flew to the left and hit the ground hard. She turned to look back at him, her lip bleeding and a tear on her cheek.

"You guys want me to take care of this family, but all you guys do is oppose me! I'm fixing this once and for all!" Ryder grabbed his keys and started for the front door.

Karen yelled, "Ryder! Don't!"

The Nissan Altima was squealing out of the driveway heading west, toward Jeremy's house.

Chapter Forty-One

It was lightly sprinkling outside, which was a nice relief from the monsoon season downpours that had been pelting the area lately. This time of the afternoon, there was always a lull in Becky's television schedule, so she decided to turn on the stereo and go downstairs to start some laundry.

Ryder yelled, "Get your ass out here, Mr. Milkman! We have some talking to do! Ha!"

Being downstairs with the stereo on, Becky had not heard the yelling. She was lightly humming to the music and milling about with her laundry. Separating the different colors and applying stain-remover to some garments.

"Come on out!" Ryder yelled even louder, "Are you afraid?" He reached down and picked up a baseball-size rock, throwing it at the front bay window. The toss was too light as it hit the siding below the window. "Get out here, you wimp!"

Troy had heard the loud *crack* of the rock and stepped over to look out of his window. There was a dark grey Nissan Altima in front of the Hardners' home, with a man standing outside of it, shaking his fist and yelling towards the home.

Becky had also heard the loud *crack*. Coming up the stairs to investigate, she saw a man out front, yelling at her home. She muttered, "My word, what is going on?" and watched as the man reached down, picked something up and hurled it towards the house. There was a loud *crack* on the front door this time.

She said to herself, "Why, you son of a bitch!" Then reached over, picking up the phone to call the police. No dial tone; it was dead. Becky had not bought into the cell phone thing, believing it sucked some of your soul away. The man could see her through the window. He smiled and held up a pair of pruning shears. She was getting mad now. *He must have cut the phone lines. Well buddy I hope you like buckshot!* Becky walked back to her bedroom, pulling out the twelve-gauge shotgun from under her bed. She knew it was already loaded, didn't even bother checking.

In the meantime, Troy had called Jesse, who was at home putting stuff away from the move. He answered on the first ring, "Hey, Troy. What's up?"

"Jesse there is a man standing outside your mom's house, yelling at it and throwing rocks."

Jesse, a little startled, asked, "What's he driving?"

"Dark grey Nissan Altima."

"On my way! Call the police, Troy!" Jesse threw the cell phone in his pocket, grabbed his keys and headed for the Firebird at a sprint.

Becky emerged on to the front porch with what Ryder identified as a double-barreled shotgun. He had not expected this. At the same time, he heard a hot rod sliding around the corner, heading his direction. From the street light that the hot rod had just passed under, Ryder saw that it was a late model Firebird, which made him grin.

Jesse roared up the street. At the right spot he slammed on his brakes and yanked the wheel to the right. Even though it was raining, he had rolled his window down at the corner. The sideways slide brought the driver-side door right next to where Ryder was standing. As planned, Ryder came at Jesse through the window. Jesse released the door and pushed it open with all his might. The top of the door frame connected with Ryder's forehead, sending him reeling backward into his own car. This didn't slow Ryder down a bit; he was back at Jesse before he could clear the car door and slammed into it, pinning him. With a right hook to Ryder's ear, Jesse was able to free himself. Now they were both in fighting stances, each hungry for the other.

Becky had managed her way along the walkway to the driveway then about halfway down she fired the gun in the air. Ryder had his back to the house and had not been aware of Becky coming from behind.

"Stop it right now! I only have one more shot and it is going to be for your head, mister!"

Startled, Ryder jumped and ran for his own car. Jesse ran up beside him and clocked him right in the left side of his head. This made Ryder's head bounce off the top of the car but just as quickly he swung his fist back and hit Jesse right in the nose, knocking him off balance. Ryder managed to finally duck into the car, put it in drive and perform a U-turn to head back the way he had come, toward the highway.

Jesse was sitting on the ground, watching Ryder take off. Of course, Ryder showed him his middle finger. Just as the side of the trunk came even with Jesse, he heard something pounding on the inside of the trunk lid, then very audibly there was a "Help! Get me out of here!"

"Holy crap! Mom, you OK?"

"Yes, Jesse. Who was that?"

"A new friend, now go back inside and wait for the police."

"Why? I'll just shoot your friend if he comes back."

"He has his stepson in the trunk."

Jesse jumped in and spun the Firebird around, tires smoking, and was off like a rocket.

Chapter Forty-Two

John was driving home from a relaxing day of fishing; he had six pan-size rainbow trout in his cooler. Melissa promised him and Kevin a trout almandine dinner if he could bring some fish home. He had never had such a fancy-sounding meal. The radio was turned up and John was singing along to one of his favorite Lynyrd Skynyrd songs when his phone began to ring.

Turning down the stereo he muttered, "Welcome back to civilization." He picked up his phone, noticing it was Jesse.

In a distressed voice he heard Jesse ask, "Where you at?"

"Why do I have the feeling you are about to ruin my tranquil day off?"

"I am in pursuit of Ryder, west on highway 58 two miles before McIntyre. Damn accident or something, in traffic hell!"

"Funny, just passed 58, I'm not even going to ask why. Give me five."

John hung up, cussed to himself then yanked the wheel to the right, driving through the grassed median that separated the east and westbound lanes of I-70 and gunning the motor.

Jesse was at a complete stop, sitting in the fast lane. After a couple of minutes he caught something moving in his left side mirror. He turned to look back and saw a big Bronco aggressively driving up the grassed median. John came up beside Jesse, rolling his window down, "You look like you're having fun."

Jesse smiled, "About time. Don't tell me, traffic was bad?"

"So what's going on?"

"Ryder is driving that dark grey Nissan Altima about a half mile ahead."

John's Bronco being taller than most cars allowed him to see ahead. He nodded his head, "Got him!"

"Leave your cell phone on, and I believe he has someone in the trunk."

John gave Jesse a strange look then rolled up his window and gunned the Bronco. Flinging mud and grass while avoiding the occasional storm grate, he was quickly gaining on the Altima. A couple of the policemen had pointed at him when he was driving by the accident, but they did not bother giving chase. Jesse thought, *Too bad.*

Ryder was happy to see the big traffic snarl, he was not going to be able to outrun that Firebird much longer. He did manage to cut people off, raising quite the ruckus, drivers honking at him and showing him their middle fingers. All the while, he produced enough distance between him and Jesse that it was not in Jesse's interest to jump out and try to catch him on foot. Finally released from the traffic jam, Ryder started accelerating, and then he noticed a large four-wheel-drive Ford Bronco shredding grass and mud, flying up the median and dodging obstacles. The driver was looking at him as he steered the Bronco up the embankment to jump back up onto the pavement. It was coming right for him. Ryder gunned the Altima 3.5 with the V6 motor and it shot off like a rocket, but he was not widening the gap between him and the Bronco. It was right on his tail.

Jesse had lost sight of the two of them as he was waiting for the traffic to filter through the accident. For a minute, all he could hear was the roaring of the Bronco's motor. Then he heard John mutter, "Got you now, you son of a bitch." There was a loud thud and some banging around, then some tire-screeching. The roar of the motor revved up real high again for about ten seconds, and then there was the unmistakable thundering crunch of metal on metal, with more tire-screeching noises.

John said into the phone, "Got the Altima stopped, at McIntyre exit. Ryder jumped ship, running toward the old stone mill by the train yard." After putting his phone in a back pocket, he reached behind his seat, grabbing the trusty bat he called Betty and took off running in the direction Ryder had disappeared.

Chapter Forty-Three

Jesse was finally freed from the gripping confines of traffic, dropping the Firebird into second gear and slamming the gas pedal to the floor. Fishtailing for a few seconds before the tires grabbed the pavement and the car shot forward. He blew by several cars immediately, having to move over into the merge to avoid the slower-moving cars. The next exit was McIntyre. He could see no evidence of any stopped cars on the ramp. Once he got to the top, he saw the Bronco to the left, on the south side of the over-pass bridge. As he pulled up to the scene the Bronco was sitting sideways in front of the Nissan, whose hood was pinned underneath the Bronco. Jesse muttered, "He kept the trunk in mind."

Jesse said loudly, "Hello! Anyone around?"

The pounding on the inside of the trunk lid started again. Jesse went to open the driver-side door and found it locked. "Really, he took the time to…" He looked around on the ground, found a softball-size rock, took four steps back then flung the rock at the side window. It cracked in a spider-web formation. He lifted his foot, kicking out the window and reaching in to find the trunk release. Gary pushed the trunk open, looking over the lid to see who was there, hoping it was not Ryder.

"You. The milkman."

"Yep. Are you ok, Gary?"

"I think so."

"Crawl in that Bronco and get out of the rain. If I'm not back in an hour, there is a gas station a few blocks north."

"OK."

Jesse sprinted in the direction John had told him. The light in the sky was starting to slowly fade now. Right when the train yard came into view on the other side of the creek, he saw two muzzle flashes with their reports following. .

"Damnit."

He searched the north side of the creek, looking up then down the embankment, *How did they cross?* Then he spotted an old rail bridge that spanned the river. He ran as fast as he could through the rocks and willows, not slowing for a moment, even when he reached the bridge. There was no time.

A minute later, the train yard came into view. Jesse slowed to a jog so he could hear better while surveying the area. Then he heard some loud arguing, which seemed to be coming from one of the railcars. He looked in several of them before he finally heard some more arguing, behind him now. Turning around, he saw a tall cylinder-shaped concrete building that must have had a relatively small interior, right next to the creek. On the exterior there were ladders and catwalks on all sides. Due to where the creek was, Jesse had to grab hold of the ladder attached to the ground and hang over a steep embankment to see the side where the noises were coming from. Ryder was holding a small-frame revolver at his side and John was standing about ten feet away, with Betty in hand.

John put Betty in his back waist-band and rushed Ryder. Ryder readjusted, aiming at John and firing three rapid shots. Jesse saw some red liquid fly out the back of John's right side, but it didn't seem to slow him down. John hit Ryder with his right shoulder lifted up and slammed him against the concrete silo. He was beating Ryder with his fists, but then somehow the gun materialized again. John saw it in the nick of time, jumping to the left, or Ryder would have had him dead to rights.

Unfortunately in the dark, John couldn't have seen that the platform ended, and he fell silently into the rushing current of Clear Creek. The recent heavy rains had swelled the river and John was swept quickly downstream. Jesse lost his friend's head bobbing in the water within seconds because of the speed he was whisked away. He wanted to yell out to John, to dive in to help, but that would only reveal his position to Ryder. Besides, at this point, there was nothing he could do to help John; they would both be in the same boat, leaving Gary completely exposed.

Jesse watched as Ryder started making his way back down and decided to surprise him once he got back on the ground. There was an old, weak metal door, with a deep frame where he could hide in the shadows, right next to the ladder base. He started counting back the shots; there had been five so far that he knew of. *Was that small frame revolver big enough to hold six?*

Ryder's feet came into view as he was climbing down the last section of ladder. He jumped off the last rung then out of the shadows Jesse charged and tackled Ryder onto the hard ground. Jesse rose up, sitting on Ryder's stomach and clocking him with two hard punches to the head before Ryder bucked him off. Jesse rolled over and came to his feet at lightning speed. Ryder was dazed and did not get up fast enough; he was on all fours when

Jesse kicked him in the side, hearing ribs crack as Ryder flew a couple of feet and landed on his stomach. Jesse ran up to make the same move but Ryder grabbed his foot, pulling hard, which made Jesse lose balance and fall over the top of Ryder. Jesse rolled into a somersault, coming to his feet instantly. Ryder was up, standing in a fighting stance, waiting for the next move.

Jesse walked directly at him with his hands down. The second he was in range, Ryder threw his right fist at Jesse's nose, only to have it blocked to the side with a very quick arm then a foot planted right on his sternum. Ryder flipped backwards and smashed into the old metal door. The latch had given in and the door flew open.

Ryder quickly crawled inside, slamming the door shut. Jesse heard a *click* from the other side. He walked up; trying the handle, but it was locked. Looking around, there was nothing useful to pry the door open. He pushed on the door to test its strength.

"What the hell!" He walked twenty feet away from the door then turned around and rushed it, staying low. His shoulder hit it about mid-height as he lifted at the same time and the door gave in. Rolling to a stop in the middle of the concrete room, he looked around for Ryder and with the door open now he was able to catch the gleaming stainless steel of a gun barrel. He got up to run back outside when there was a deafening roar inside the small chamber. Jesse felt the bullet hit, just grazing his upper arm and pushing through some meat on his left shoulder. It spun him around backward, to the ground. Jesse had forgotten about the gun or he would have crossed the threshold differently.

Jesse knew he had to ignore and fight through this pain; Ryder was not just going to leave matters be and go home. Somehow, Ryder had also managed to come across a foot-long blue breaker bar and before he could stand back up Jesse felt the breaker bar hit his right side. If he fell back to the ground he was dead. Jesse managed to push hard with his right arm, to bring himself into a standing position, facing Ryder. They were both getting tired and a little more sluggish. Ryder raised his arm with the bar in it, coming down fast and hard, Jesse managing to feign to the right, grabbing Ryder's elbow and helping it continue its arc, hitting Ryder in the knee. He let out a yell, dropping to the ground, but keeping hold of the breaker bar. Jesse kicked him in the same side he had before, which rolled Ryder over onto his back. Jesse had him right where he wanted and thought, *Finally this is going to end and none too soon.*

Suddenly, the gleaming barrel was back in play, pointing directly at Jesse's face not more than five feet away. Jesse thought as he reeled backwards, *Did he have time to reload?* Ryder laughed then threw the gun at Jesse. Before Jesse could stop himself, he slammed into a metal pipe sticking out of the wall, knocking the wind out of him. Now Ryder was up, charging with the blue bar. Jesse was caught twice, once on each side, before he was able to push him off. This caused a massive amount of pain. Nearly losing consciousness, Jesse shook his head, breathing deeply to try to stave off the blackness.

Ryder was limping around the concrete room, swinging the blue breaker bar that he had hit Jesse with a dozen times. He was confident he had Jesse beaten and could finish him off with little effort.

"This is what happens, Jesse, when you go and mess with another man's family."

Jesse was kneeling on the ground in the middle of the small concrete room, beaten pretty hard. Gunshot wound through his shoulder; ribs aching from the breaker bar; multiple cuts on his arms, and one bleeding pretty steadily on his shoulder. While kneeling, he was trying to catch his breath so he could fend off this maniac once he resumed his attack.

"You don't have a family. You have some unwilling prisoners." Jesse twisted in

pain to get a better view of his assailant, "I
haven't figured out why they stay yet."

"My family loves me."

"What are you going to do with Gary?"

"He's not family, just a stepson."

"And a nephew. You don't consider that
family?"

Ryder was surprised by how much Jesse
knew, "I denounced the Hamlins as my family.
They were too dysfunctional."

Jesse laughed a little, but it hurt his side,
"Do you hear yourself?"

"That's enough chit-chat for me. I'm really
sorry to do this to you. You seem like a nice guy
and all. This was supposed to be Doug, but he
went and got himself put in jail, so you'll do fine
until he gets out."

"You got the talkin' part done, Ryder.
Bring it!"

Ryder got the breaker bar ready and began
his approach, "Bet you wish your buddy was
here now and didn't have that unfortunate
tumble into the creek. HA!"

Jesse watched Ryder's face drop from a
menacing smirk into fear as from behind him a
gravely unmistakable voice said, "Oh, his buddy
is here."

Ryder turned to see John holding Betty,
dripping wet from head to toe, standing in the
door-way. His shoulders were wide and his
eyes like a demon's; flat-out scary to look at.

Ryder let out a yell and ran right at John, raising the breaker bar as high as he could. John ducked low to the right, swinging Betty hard and connecting with Ryder's knee. Ryder let out a yell and dropped the bar as he was going down. Before Ryder collided with the floor John kicked out his left heel and delivered a devastating blow to the side of Ryder's left temple. Ryder landed like a bag of rocks, completely unconscious. It was over that quick.

Jesse watched the finish, then fell to his right without even trying to slow his descent, passing out from sheer exhaustion and a probable concussion. John ran over, kneeling next to his buddy, and felt his strong pulse. Jesse looked bad; he had taken quite the beating. By the look of Ryder, he had delivered one too. John saw his friend had also been shot. He tore off his shirt and made a crude tourniquet to hopefully stop the shoulder from bleeding. Once the task was complete, he felt into his friend's front pocket and found the zip-ties he knew Jesse would be carrying. John zipped two of them together then grabbed Ryder by the back of his belt and dragged him over next to the wall, where there were several pipes jutting out of the floor. He pulled Ryder's arms behind his back and secured him to a metal pipe.

Once John had successfully escaped the relentless river current, he had tried his phone to call Detective Gomez for some help, but it was soaked and would not even turn on. Walking back over he retrieved Jesse's phone, but the screen was shattered and it would not turn on, either. Back to Ryder, John felt around in his pockets and pulled out an old flip-phone that sprung to life when opened. *Hmm, something to be said for these.* However, as with most people these days, he could not recall the actual number, usually being able to summon it from the phone's memory. He dialed 9-1-1.

Chapter Forty-Four

Edward spoke into the radio attached to his chest as he was barreling down I-70 eastbound, lights flashing and siren howling, "Hey Connie, this is Edward."

"Hi Edward, what do you need?"

"You have two arrivals coming in. I need you at the first one."

"Why? It's Raven's night to assist the gurneys."

"Just trust me. Can you give Raven something else to do for a few minutes?"

Edward pulled in, slammed the gear shift into park then jumped out to assist the medic with opening the door and dropping the gurney onto the concrete path. Connie was standing at the back of the ambulance with a doctor dressed in a white lab coat. Once the gurney was freed and being wheeled inside, Connie looked at the patient that the doctor was testing vitals on as the gurney rolled into the ER lobby.

She looked at Edward, "Oh my!"

Edward nodded his head, "He's lost a lot of blood, the next thirty minutes are crucial."

Connie looked back at the receiving area to see a man walking under his own power, who looked like he had been through hell. Most of his shirt was in rags, it barely hung on, revealing dozens of scratches and cuts across his powerful chest. He had some cuts on his legs, too, and was not wearing any shoes. His well-muscled arms were held at his side and despite the pain he must have felt, he walked forward with a stunning confidence, following the gurney that carried Jesse.

When they got to the room where they would work on Jesse a nurse put her hand up to the man's chest to stop him from entering. John looked to see a friendly face say, "He's going to be well taken care of in there, honey," She pointed to the room next door, "Now let's get you into this room to look at your array of injuries."

John followed her into the room and sat heavily down on the bed. He was exhausted from his turbulent fight with Clear Creek. He had been slammed into rocks and trees, pushed over a ten-foot waterfall and nearly drowned a dozen times trying to escape the raging current. John remembered losing his shoes in the mud near the river's edge when he finally found a handhold that didn't break off.

There were two nurses tending to his many scrapes, cuts and where the bullet had grazed his right mid-section. He vaguely remembered one of the nurses threading a needle before he fell to his side on the bed and passed out.

After Jesse had been stabilized and was receiving blood, Connie felt guilty and texted Raven, *'Can you meet me in the ER lobby?'*

"Yes."

Raven figured she needed help cleaning a room up or stitching a patient, but she noticed Connie had a very agitated look about her.

"What's up, Connie?"

"Raven, come with me," Connie said as she slid her arm under Raven's and walked with her.

Raven knew something was wrong. Connie had never done this with her and she was trying to think what it could be. All kinds of horrible scenarios played through her head, except the one that she walked up to. His head was turned a little; she could tell he was sleeping.

She started running into the room, "Oh my god, Jesse!"

Raven looked his body over; he had bandages and bruising all over. He was being given blood and there also seemed to be what looked like a stitched-up gunshot wound on his shoulder. She started shaking while she examined each machine, to make sure it was functioning correctly and that all the signs were in the safe zone.

Connie saw that she had some tears developing, so she stepped in to help calm her down.

"Raven, he is going to be just fine. Make sure he finishes those antibiotics. As young and strong as he is, I bet he is walking around in two weeks."

Chapter Forty-Five

John heard the door to his hospital room open and his dad's voice quietly asked Melissa about his status.

Melissa sighed, "He has not woken up yet, but the doctor said he should be just fine, barring any infection to the gunshot wound."

John slowly came to life, hemming and hawing, then asked Melissa as he faked grasping for breath, "Melissa, where are you? I have one last request." He let that hang in the air for a minute as he had everyone's full worried attention. Then he smiled, "There are some trout in the Bronco. Can you go rescue them and stick them in the freezer?"

Melissa slapped John's shoulder, "Would you quit scaring me?"

Kevin giggled, "Where's the Bronco?"

"I think you'll have to ask Gomez. I was brought here in a different manner."

Suddenly, John sat up, "Where's Jesse?"

"Whoa, slow down there, cowboy," Kevin said as he stepped over to stop his son from standing up. "He's next door, doing just fine."

John visibly relaxed, "Can we go see him?"

"Of course, but let's take it slowly, I just walked by and saw he was awake. Becky's there, too."

"Oh great! I better cover up my underwear."

John shuffled into Jesse's room to see him alert, talking with his mom and Raven, "Hey, Sweetpea!"

Jesse replied, "Ah, Honey Bear, how you doing?" These were the nicknames they assigned to each other many years ago but rarely used these days.

The room filled with cheerful banter and laughter. Jesse had a hard time laughing too much with three broken ribs so he kept trying to hold back. After a few minutes of catching up, Becky stepped up to John, smiled at him and gave him a big hug.

She had a tear in her eye, "Thank you for saving my boy, John."

He smiled, "I didn't want to have to start mowing yours and Raven's lawn too, so I figured this was the best alternative."

Melissa slapped his shoulder and that got the laughter rolling again.

Kevin interrupted, "How do I find this 'Gomez' so I can retrieve John's truck?"

Raven answered as she was tending to one of Jesse's many cuts, "I already asked, because you know who was worried about his precious Firebird. The police towed them to the station, they are in the impound lot, but are free to be retrieved."

"I'll grab Steve, we'll go get it."

Raven asked, "Mr. Rodney, can you grab someone else too, and get Jesse's Firebird? I'd like to stay here."

"Oh sweet, that's the one I'm driving!"

Chapter Forty-Six

Detectives Gomez and Singer joined the
congregation in Jesse's hospital room the next
morning. Since the rooms were built for two
patients, the staff had moved John in to share
now that they were both on the mend. As long
as their conditions continued to improve, John
was slated to be released in two days and Jesse
the day after.

Once the idle chit-chat and introductions
died down Gomez said, "So, would everybody
like a debriefing?"

The room went silent and all eyes were
focused intently on the detective, "This is a
pretty strange story. By the way, before I start,
Ryder is on this same floor at the end of the hall.
He is handcuffed to the gurney, which is
chained up in a secure fashion."

Everyone looked around at each other, but
nobody said anything.

"So everybody knows that Ryder, formerly Harry, and Doug are brothers, right? And that Gary is Doug's son, being raised by his uncle that married his biological father's ex-wife?"

Again, Gomez looked around the room; he got a couple of nods of agreement.

"Doug and Harry were born to a Nick and Wanda Hamlin. Wanda had been married previously to an Army veteran that was killed overseas. Together, they had a son named, Terry. It seems that the Hamlin boys' father had treated the stepson in the same fashion that Ryder had been treating his stepson, Gary. He almost acts as if he has done nothing wrong. Stating that his father did a 'fine job' raising them," Gomez used his fingers as quotes then paused for a second. "I guess the apple doesn't fall far from the tree in this case."

Gomez looked over at Jesse and then to John, "Ryder had led you two guys back to where his stepbrother Terry was killed. They used to play among the railcars, sometimes pretending to be hobos and practicing their skills at jumping onto a moving train. One time, the older brother was not as fortunate. He slipped underneath and was cut in two by a train. From the point of view that Harry had, he always blamed his brother Doug for Terry's death. Harry's revenge was going to be on Doug's son in the end."

Gomez stopped for a second to let that sink in, "I confirmed these facts with Doug. Who, by the way, ended up dropping his state-appointed attorney and pled his own case to the judge. This is not a recommended practice. But in this case it worked; Doug won his freedom from most of his priors, he just has to serve a few more days in jail. Singer and I were present and he called upon us as character witnesses. Jack was also subpoenaed and he confirmed that Doug had saved him from what could have been an extreme beating. Gary and Karen were present, but they were not called to the stand. However, I am not sure if the judge was afraid of Doug or legitimately felt for him."

Gomez had stopped talking and everyone else was silent, thinking the story through.

Out of the blue there was the sound of small, running pitter-patter steps. Jesse looked over to see Haylee running to him, Karen and Gary not far behind. She stopped by his bedside and gave him a big hug around the neck, "I knew you could do it, Jesse."

"Hi, Haylee. How are you today?"

She stepped back and smiled at him, "I'm sad about my dad going away for a while, but we talked with him and he's gonna get better now."

Chapter Forty-Seven

Raven generally went grocery shopping for the whole week on Friday mornings. Since Jesse was not at work but at home recovering, this time he decided to join her. He felt pain with just about any movement that he made but he was sick and tired of being stuck inside the house.

Raven asked, "Are you sure you can walk that far?"

"I'm going to give it a try. If I don't make it, just drag me over into the sun and leave me be."

Jesse started to get up off the couch, making funny grunts and groans from the aches and pains that were stabbing at his nerves. He was slow and clumsy, trying to avoid more shooting pains.

"Oh, silly, here, let me help you get up."

After he got to a standing position, walking was not as painfully difficult. Raven had never driven a stick shift before, so John had taught her just two days' prior, in Jesse's car. Needless to say, she was not very smooth with the shifting and each time she had to, the jarring jolt would send more searing flashes of pain through his sides. He remained quiet, trying to hold back his grimaces.

The King Soopers grocery store where Raven shopped had a few other retail outlets attached. It was a strip-mall theme with the grocery store as the anchor. One of the shops was named Pet Ranch.

As they walked by the pet store, Jesse said, "I'm gonna go in here for a minute."

"Ok, I'm going to head on to King's and start the grocery shopping. Pick up Rio something nice."

"I'll catch up with you." Jesse said as he pushed open the door to the pet store. He started milling around, looking at the different options for Frisbees, Rio's favorite pastime. The reptiles always interested him, but he would not want one for a pet. Near the back was a six-plex of glass enclosures. Inside each was a different type of dog. On the bottom right was a little pup with a very distinctive mask; a half-white, half-tan muzzle and a black head. His body was painted like a black-and-white cow. He was staring at Jesse, wagging his tail and looked to almost be smiling; a very happy boy.

The only clerk in the store was up front, helping another customer gather grasshoppers to feed her snake. Jesse walked past the 'Employees Only' sign, then painfully sat down on the floor and opened the pup's cage. He came running out, jumping in Jesse's lap and licking his face. Jesse fell in love with the little guy immediately. He didn't put him back in the cage; instead, he carried him out to the leash aisle and found one that fit him perfectly.

The store clerk smiled at Jesse, "I figured that little guy would go quickly. We only got him in yesterday."

Jesse put the leash over the pup's head in a slip-knot fashion. He picked out a couple of bowls, some food and a box of dog biscuits.

"He's a puppy. You're probably going to want a couple of chew toys."

Jesse had his hands full, so the clerk stepped over and grabbed a couple off the shelf, "These ones will work."

"Throw in one of those Frisbees too." Jesse settled with the pet shop clerk, "Can you hold on to him for just a minute?"

"Sure."

Jesse noticed somebody had abandoned a grocery cart just outside the pet store. Wheeling it in, he loaded it up with his supplies, including the dog. As he started pushing the cart the little pup ran to the front and stood up by bracing his feet on the top of the cart, to watch where they were headed. He was quite the hit with the kids in the grocery store as Jesse wheeled the pup along, looking down each aisle for Raven. She had her back to him, looking at the different salsa options on the shelf.

"I got Rio something I think he is really going to like."

Raven kept searching through the jars, "That's nice, honey."

Finally finding the item that had been eluding her, she grabbed it and turned around, "Oh my, he is gorgeous," she smiled at Jesse after kissing the pup, "an executive decision, I take it?"

"Umm, yes, I hope that's ok."

"This time it is. I'm done, let's get him home."

They sat around after dinner, playing with the new pup, trying to think of a name for him.

Raven said, "I've got it. How about Jericho?"

"That's a great name. Hey, Jericho. Come here, boy."

ABOUT THE AUTHOR

Greg Buck lives with his wife Lori and three dogs in Westminster, Colorado. This is his second book and the second book of The Milkman series.

Made in the USA
Las Vegas, NV
24 December 2020

14741604R00196